FIELD LANE

FIELD LANE

A NOVEL BY

JOHN SODEAU

Copyright © 2024 John Sodeau

The moral right of the author has been asserted.

Apart from any fair dealing for the purposes of research or private study, or criticism or review, as permitted under the Copyright, Designs and Patents Act 1988, this publication may only be reproduced, stored or transmitted, in any form or by any means, with the prior permission in writing of the publishers, or in the case of reprographic reproduction in accordance with the terms of licences issued by the Copyright Licensing Agency. Enquiries concerning reproduction outside those terms should be sent to the publishers.

This is a work of fiction. Names, characters, businesses, places, events and incidents are either the products of the author's imagination or used in a fictitious manner. Any resemblance to actual persons, living or dead, or actual events is purely coincidental.

Troubador Publishing Ltd
Unit E2 Airfield Business Park,
Harrison Road, Market Harborough,
Leicestershire LE16 7UL
Tel: 0116 279 2299
Email: books@troubador.co.uk
Web: www.troubador.co.uk

ISBN 978 1 80514 235 5

British Library Cataloguing in Publication Data.
A catalogue record for this book is available from the British Library.

Printed and bound in Great Britain by 4edge Limited
Typeset in 11pt Minion Pro by Troubador Publishing Ltd, Leicester, UK

For Fran and Harry

Preface

> "Unfortunately, in a global economic system dominated by profit, new forms of slavery have developed, in a certain way worse and more inhuman than those of the past."
> *Pope Francis, April 2015*

> "Only those who are color blind speak of black and white."
> *Giovannie de Sadeleer*

Field Lane is a book about a place where real-world people meet established fictional characters and newly imagined ones. It is a literary crossover telling a metaphysical story behind the stories of some well-loved classics set in London by the Thames and along the Mississippi.

The novel is set in the 1800s with all that century's prejudices about race, religion and gender playing a central part in people's lives. Therefore, the language employed in the text reflects that time: *Lector cavē*.

October 2023

Prologue

"God save the Queen. The King is dead."

It is June 1837 and William IV, ex-naval officer, ex-Duke of Clarence and father of numerous illegitimate children has died of a heart attack.

It is said.

The now Dowager Queen Consort, Adelaide of Saxe-Meiningen, was lost and confused. Partly because of her need for the medications that she had been increasingly using over the past two years. But mainly because she was not sure if she was pregnant or not.

"All I want is a long life," she muttered to herself when told the news of her late husband. She was only thirty-nine years old, after all.

There was a large age difference between William and herself. Until one hour ago, he had been seventy-two years old and had always enjoyed his increasingly occasional marital benefits, as he loved to say. It had always been so with him. Countless seed of his were sown in the West Indies when he served in the Royal Navy.

Countless "little monkeys", as he called them, ran around there due to his attentions. All born with no regrets, indeed, no actual thoughts ever about them.

Then again, there were his eleven illegitimate children and the royal five of her own with him who had all miscarried or died.

For the less direct line of William, their careful plans for a chosen successor would be torn apart if Adelaide were pregnant.

Princess Alexandrina Victoria of Kent would not then be anointed, and a future suitable German consort could never exist.

No, it was thought, Queen Victoria must come next, whatever it took.

I

Innocence

Charley Boats

When I was working for the best-known pickpocketing gang in London, I never thought I'd become a grazier in Northamptonshire. Mainly because I had no idea what the word grazier meant or where Northamptonshire even was.

Me, a lad from Wapping in the East End, breathing in the fresh air, fattening sheep for market and making a good, honest living. Who would have believed it? Certainly not my dad.

And definitely not Fagin, politely known as a receiver of stolen goods. Although now, ten years later, I know he was nothing more than a thieving slaver. But you couldn't help being drawn in by him. Just like you couldn't help liking Jack Dawkins.

Most knew him as the Artful Dodger, and I remember the day when we first met by the boats at the bottom of Alderman Stairs in St Katherine's, where I'd been helping my dad on the wherry for some pennies. I probably fell in love with him on the spot with his strange eyes, snub nose and grown up, messed up clothes that were too big for him. Then there was the battered old hat.

"Get a move on," my dad shouted at me as I jumped off our wherry, tied the rope and helped the passengers off. I was relieved it was the last crossing of the morning for me. Now I could do whatever I wanted. Just then, Peter Goods' nooner from Butlers Wharf tied up next to us and this small lad about my age jumped off, took a look at me and said, "Who's a pretty boy then?"

I blushed all over and stuttered out, "None of your business."

He winked, straightened his silly hat and bounced up the stairs. "Aren't you coming too?" he called back, and I was hooked like one of the few salmon left swimming in the Thames. I knew he was going to be my best covey all within a minute.

We walked a bit towards the Tower of London and laughed and talked about things like his friend Nancy and what she did. I told him about the Southwark whorehouses where most of our passengers went to visit. He said he had been running an errand for his guv'nor.

"No idea what I was carrying, as always. Beyond my apprehension. Nice, vocable crib by St Saviours Dock though. Don't like him much but he pays well for an ugly chazer."

We both thought we were about ten years old. He seemed older than me, though. He definitely used fancier words. Sometimes I had no idea what he was saying. Then out of the blue he said, "Fancy a trip up West?"

And that was the start of a new life for me. Not a great start, I admit, because walking through the smelly brown "mud" that was the streets and breathing in the yellowish, choking fog which smelt of bad eggs and stung the eyes was not my idea of a top afternoon. But there's no doubt London has some great sights to see, despite the smoke thrown up into the air by the dirty chimneys. The Bloody Tower, Traitors' Gate, The Great Fire Monument and the newly opened London Bridge right in front of it. And then St Paul's Cathedral. Seeing it all made me proud to be an Englishman just like Grandad Jimmy was always telling me to be.

The next hour or so seemed like ten minutes on the walk with Jack. We only stopped to get a couple of penny muttons from one of the pie men in West Street. And just after that, we got to the narrowest of alleyways just off Holborn Hill (a bit too close to the Old Black Dog, Newgate, for my liking). At the time I never knew that a house on this dirty alley would become a second home for me.

It was the stink that hit me first. Yes, I know old London Town stinks, because I live by the side of the Thames and cross it daily with its dead rats, dogs and cats floating on by. But I'm not a-kidding you when I say sheep with worms, on the farm I've worked on for years now, smell better than that midden with walls did.

These days I laugh because the filthy door Jack took me to – the boy who became a grazier – was in a place called Field Lane.

We went inside along a maze of passageways and after a few minutes he said, "I've brought you to meet a gentleman. He's called Fagin and I think he's going to like you. So, what's your real name my pretty wherry boy?"

I smiled and said, "What I told you is true... everyone calls me Charley the Boat."

I can't say the place my own family called home was a palace, but this dirty, dismal, dreary hole was something else. Hardly any light could get in from outside, and for the first time I thought to myself: *why did I do this?* I knew, of course, but I'd have to leave soon because my father would whip me bad if I didn't turn up at the Stairs in time for the evening rush on the *Rose*.

I turned round to go, and bang in front of me was a very old, very ugly man with a bit of red hair stuck on top. His beard was filthy. And I know all breath smells, but this was pure animal. He lifted his leg and let one fly.

"So then, Charley the Boat? That won't do at all, my dear. You'll be Charley Boats in the gang. And very good you're going to be, too, playing the handkerchief game, especially as the Dodger will show you first how to lift and then he'll make you happy."

I looked to Dodge. He looked down. I looked for the door and with a silent prayer hoped I could find my way out of this Heaven that was Hell.

John Boats:
aka Johnny the Boat

When I was a boy, my old man, Jimmy, was a wherryman like his dad and his dad before him. It wasn't a great life, but we were free and fit and fed. Lucky I'm here though, because both of Dad's brothers had been pressed into the Royal Navy for the American War and never came back. Silly sods. Dad somehow missed the recruitment, the sly old dog. He never said how. I never asked.

But I wouldn't be surprised if it hadn't been something to do with his sideline of ferrying important nobs and personages to prime sites for viewing the hangings and cagings of convicted pirates and maritime murderers at Execution Dock in Wapping. Those days are pretty much gone now, but other earners are possible. Don't I know it.

It's what life is all about really. Lucky accidents given a boot up the arse by knowing the right person and helping the right people, as well as getting a bit of learning in, like my dad made sure I did. Just like his dad before him.

Today isn't tomorrow, and I think the steamboats are going to be a big part of my son Charley's life in the future. No more rowing or oars for him. Lucky Charley.

He likes changes, anyway. He's a good boy but sometimes I have to give him a whack when he goes off into his dream world and forgets to do things, especially those he's not too keen on. Lilian thinks there's something a bit "off" with him, as she puts it. I know what she means, but we never talk about it.

As long as Charley is happy and doesn't break the law – especially Maritime Law – we'll love and support him. Can't believe I'm saying that, knowing some of the tricks I get up to with thieving traders down at the docks, bringing ships from the West Indies carrying sugar, rum and, more sickeningly, human parts for medicinal purposes. But the extra keeps Lil happy. And then she makes me happy too.

Frederick:
Apothecary's son

I've been trading in ointments, tallow creams and perfumed soaps in Gower Street, close to the new London University, since my father, William, passed the business on to me in 1820. He is still alive and active with his Worshipful Society of Apothecaries in Blackfriars, and also the Linnean Society where his natural history friends meet regularly. He also spends a lot of his time down at the Physic Garden in Chelsea, although not quite as much as he spends in White's in St James. He tells Mother that it is necessary for our business to meet royalty like the Prince Regent and the Dukes Clarence and Cumberland. I'm not so sure. It is, after all, a Tory meeting place with extreme ideas about the way a modern world should be run.

"And run by White's men, of course," Father told me once with a smile on his face.

Then there's the gambling, too.

Anyway, I still have no interest in any of his talking shops and amusements, as long as it keeps him from interfering with me.

I also dispense medicines, mainly herbal, and some spices, all often ineffective. Although some of the more exotic herb remedies from China can be effective against conditions like diarrhoea. Initially, I was sceptical about stocking viper bile and rattlesnake skin, but they do appear to have some beneficial effect on males with tumescence problems. I also sell more sensitive goods like opium mixtures from behind the counter because it's frowned upon by many of the clientele we serve. We got into this opium and exotics trade partly because Father acted for the Royal African Company trading triangle between London Docks, the West African Coast and the Americas. Everything is for sale.

Actually, Papa did rather more than act for the RAC, he showed them how to keep the gunpowder that they traded for slaves from blowing up. Many consignments had exploded and sunk the ships they were travelling on. But he knew that slow mixing very pure, dry ingredients in the absolutely correct proportions ensured the quality of our finest unguents – and so it proved with the gunpowder being transported from London to Africa.

Under the counter, without Papa's knowledge, I act as a middleman for my half-brother, Bill. With him, I ask no questions because I would get no answers.

We no longer deal in live human cargo, as my father used to put it, but we do purvey "slave-fat" to select (meaning, rich) clients. I'm lucky – I get the prime of the prime delivered to me because of our long-standing connections with the RAC and my contacts in the West India Docks. You'd be surprised at the profits you make with this stuff. It's actually beyond me why the aristocracy cannot get enough of it.

In case you don't know, it's used for preventing wounds from becoming infected and, most importantly, is useful for the older lady. They say it works its magic on very wrinkled skin, no matter where it is, all over the body.

The human fats mined from plantation slaves (especially Jamaican) are regarded as the most exclusive and effective because they come from bodies that have suffered badly, and so are thought much better than anything you could buy from places like effete Paris.

I often laugh to myself about the abolitionists who got the slave trade banned about thirty years ago. They were so well-meaning and earnest, but they never could really stop the triangle linking ammunitions and gunpowder to slaves, and slaves to rum and sugar. Worse, they never understood there was both a live slave trade and a dead one.

Plantations will always cry out for strong native men and women who can be worked until they drop. But the part they play in the trade triangle is not over then. The body fat from the slave corpses is carved off, rendered down and packed up for transport to England. As the Duke of C puts it every time he makes a purchase, "No wastage with the Negro. A perfect economic cycling of resources."

I don't agree with him, but I don't contradict either. Otherwise, nobody would buy from me. And I couldn't live with myself if Sykes & Son went out of business.

Charley Bates

I got home at about six, just in time to help get the first passengers on board for their night across the water. I realise now that I wasn't exactly sure what they did over there or what a prostitute actually did to them. Dodger said he knew, but he didn't explain it very well.

I messed up a couple of fares and my dad gave me one of his evil looks. But I didn't care because my mind was on the Dodge.

As you can work out by now, I actually escaped the cesspit in Field Lane. I also promised myself I wouldn't go back. Even though I knew I would and probably the next day, too. Just to see him. Not to play the handkerchief 'game', though. What would Dad say, let alone Lil, if I broke the law?

Tomorrow was my day off – even though I never get a day off, but anyway, I'd take it and risk a slap. It would be worth it just for one more look.

"Wery wherry pretty," he'd called me as I went out of the cesspit door. Well, he's not too pretty himself, that's for sure, but for some reason I'd still like to touch his face.

Off to Field Lane again. But what then? I thought I'd just hang around on the off-chance Dodger was around too. Home by eleven was what I thought. I was right, but twelve hours after my guess. Because a lot happened.

Jack always had a seventh sense. He just knew what people were going to do, and what they were going to do after that. Later, he told me he was sure I'd be back, and I'd hang around The One Tun where there was safety in numbers. And he knew I was no fool. He's right. I'm not. At least, I wasn't until I met him.

"Lesson number one," he said.

"I came here for fun, not school." I laughed back.

He snorted. "School can be fun with the right teacher."

I knew what he meant from his sly smile.

Teach me, Dodge, teach me, I thought.

"That old farshtunkener Fagin wants a Belcher today, and you're going to get it for him."

"Look I'm not in the gang of that living corpse. I'm a waterman. I get all the excitement I need by keeping out of the way of the fingers of some of our passengers on the *Rose* every night. But Dad says I'm good for business and to stop moaning. 'God rest your mother's soul', he says, every time we set off."

Jack told me there would be no fingers today unless I wanted one, or maybe two. I shrugged and smiled. And so, after a bit, we were off to the stalls down Leather Lane, where there'd be good hunting, he told me.

I spend a lot of time with perfumed old coves dressed to the nines. All with a handkerchief of one sort or another.

Meaning, I knew what a Belcher was. Mainly a light blue silk with white dots and a dark blue spot in the centre. Named after Jem himself, who Dad had met and called the best fighter ever. Everyone wanted one, but few had the coin. I could see why Fagin wanted one for his collection.

Finally, after three hours of wandering around, two possibles came into the market at the same time. One looked like a boxer; the other a bit ancient, looking at shoe buckles. Obvious anyway, which one to pick, and it was all over in a flash with the Belcher slipped in my side pocket after Dodge had nudged the old boy from right to left and then did the dip.

We were on our way. All a let-down, really. No shouting or screaming, just the two of us on the road to the cesspit.

"Charley Bates, if I'm not mistaken, my dear – and I never am," said Fagin, another three hours later when I gave him the Belcher.

I looked at Dodge. He looked down. I looked for the door and realised, like it or not, that I had a new name and was in Fagin's gang.

"Same time next week," said Jack. It wasn't a question. "I'll show you some real fun then."

John Boats:
Mr Laudanum

More and more Chinese seamen were coming into the London Docks areas, especially Limehouse. A bit too close to St Katherine's for my liking, as they wanted our women. And that's not right. Keep to your own lot, and your gambling and opium. And they could be cruel and violent when the mood took them. No, not for me.

But they knew how to trade alright. For that, they needed locals to change their drugs into good hard coin. That's where I could offer my services, because all three sides of the trading triangle going between Africa, the Americas and the London Docks loved the poppy whatever it was mixed with, from a cuppa tea to a splash of Old Toms.

My old man, Jimmy, had contacts everywhere from a life lived on the Thames just this side of the law. The tradesmen, the skippers, the crooks and, most of all, the 'nobbery', as he called them. The most important of them to me was some toff called William Sykes, who was an apothecary and had a lot of influence in the Royal African Company – the slavers, as I knew them when I was only an innocent boy. Although Rose would never have agreed with me ever being described as fuckin' innocent.

Sykes had known my father from the trading market in Greenwich, where he ferried the slaves from the Docks. His boy was about the same age as me so, although I'd never met him, I had heard of Frederick Sykes and what he did for a living. Working in his father's business. Just like me.

Our own business together started in late 1830, ten years after he was given the shop like I was given a boat.

I asked the old man if he could get me a proper introduction with him and he said yes. It wasn't as big a thing as it sounded to me. Really, I just visited the shop in Gower Street, pushed the door open, the clapper bell rang and there was Fred standing behind an old wooden counter with shelf after shelf behind him filled with dirty coloured glass bottles and little boxes. He was taller than I expected, elegant but a bit over-scented for my taste. Maybe a Miss Molly. Good-looking, though, "Not as good-looking as you, Johnny boy," I said under my breath.

I told him who I was, but he was expecting me, obviously. Then I asked him if he ever sold medicinal potions made with opium. Straight as that.

"Of course I do, but I don't put laudanum on the counter because our clients would hate their friends to know they need the stronger poppy mixtures to calm them down. Lavender and chamomile are much more acceptable in their social groups."

Straightaway I could see a problem. The Limehouse dealers would not want to bother with trading small amounts of their drug to just one outlet.

"How do you increase your customers' wants then?"

"Well, that could be unethical. But the obvious way would be to increase the amount of poppy in the doses, meaning making stronger solutions. Fairly soon the client would need more and more. The trick would be to say the cravings are perfectly natural and show the opium is doing its job... and what's more, it's giving you a longer, happier life."

"Even better would be to get punters who don't need it at all to start using and then get them addicted, too," I thought out loud.

"What we need are 'Poppy shops' where people go to wind down or do business, like they do in coffee shops," I said. I'll always remember that as the moment which changed my life.

"You can mix opium with anything can't you, Fred? Alcohol, bhang, ether, datura? Why not in coffee or tea or milk?"

As soon as he said there was no reason why not, I cracked a grin and thought to myself, *that's the easy bit done, Mr Laudanum.*

Frederick Sykes

I liked Johnny. Funny. Smart. Rogue. Charm. Had them all. It was the rogue bit that worried me. Could he be like my half-brother Bill? He was definitely muscular.

Bill was a tough character, sometimes abusive. Always ready to start a fight. He was also illegitimate, the son of a prostitute my father had bedded five years after I was born. He wasn't entirely disowned, though, and was given the name Sykes, although my father did not like it one bit that his street-earning mother called him Bill. I didn't see him much because Father had forbidden me to.

But if Bill did contact me then it was generally because of something dubious, and he had to "rest" somewhere for a month or three.

I'm a pretty honest man, I think. The human fat-selling and making the opium mixtures are perfectly legal. But if Johnny and I were able to do what we planned, then untold damage to people's health might be done. Yes, some good would be coming from it, too. Life is lived at a very fast pace these days and the changes we see every day are not always welcome to the general sanguinity of people, especially the *hoi polloi*.

So, get to work, Fred.

Should I just boil up poppy seeds like a leaf tea? Or could I make a tea and poppy infusion? Would it work by boiling them with coffee grounds? Or should I just add poppy latex milk to tea or gin or whatever? And let it mature. I could start that off straight away using a bottle or two of cheap Old Tom gin and some juice or seed. Or use my high quality Ardbeg whisky from Islay. This is the part I always like when making a new ointment – the not knowing.

Father was a botanist first and a frustrated chemist second, really. He had become interested in the science of explosives while attending a discourse at the Royal Institution off Piccadilly years ago.

That's where he met John Farquhar, a very odd soul. Nobody would guess he had earnt hundreds of thousands of pounds in India helping the King of Bengal or whosoever with making pure gunpowder. He's the one who my father stole his knowledge from to help the RAC. Didn't acknowledge Farquhar, of course, but honestly that man wouldn't know tomorrow from yesterday unless it was something to do with mathematics or mechanics.

I've been frustrated with less intellectual things, too, recently. I should be married now, I know. Mother despairs when I refuse outings with one of her German *fräuleins* she introduces me to.

She had come to London with her family years ago from Hanover, with the Georgian diaspora. Her father had relatives here in the Fitzrovia area and thought he might earn more as a medical doctor than he could at home. *Die Mutter* acted as an assistant to him, mainly administering Mother's Ruin by the bottle to patients going through some painful procedure or other, and then bandaging up when the butchery was finished.

Nowadays, she spends most of her time raising funds for a new, exclusive German hospital to be built somewhere in Hackney. Charlotte Street, called locally *Charlottenstrasse*, is where she lives in a very grand house. Gower Street, where I live above the shop, is not really an important part of her life these days. Nor is William Sykes. Although it's been like that for many years now since she found out I had a half-brother. We know you were wronged, Mami, but we all are at some time or other as far as I can tell.

I've taken prostitutes, of course – like father, like son – but at thirty-five I still don't get this idea of love. Maybe my new business venture with Johnny will firework me into action. That's typical of me. Wandering my mind to put off answering the main problem we're going to have. That is, how much opium to add to make the drink addictive but not lethal. It will need to be tested on real people. But on who?

That's a bit along the line. But I do know there's lots of scum on the streets in some areas of the city. Would they really be missed if one of our tastings didn't work out?

Xie Qinggao:
The Lascar

Zhang Chen is dead. Found with his bowels ripped open. Good riddance. Shadwell will be a safer place for us all.

Ever since the East India Company dumped us into the St David's Fort Barracks, there has been trouble. Well, there were five hundred of us divided into two gang groups, all wanting the same thing. Mainly women. Sometimes boys. And always drugs. Most of the Chinese living here were peasant farmers escaping poverty and famine, while others were seamen. I was a Chenie because there were more of us. The Chin-Choo group were more violent and generally our stand-offs were stalemates.

Not last night though. All over a gambling debt of one shilling that cost the life of my closest friend from a fatal neck cut.

My name is Xie Qinggao. Been here for over five years now. So, my English is good. Means I have contacts, but I'm still as lonely, cold and out of place as I was at the start.

These days I laugh out loud about how impressed I used to be by London's wealth. Especially the buildings and, of course, the number of prostitutes. Always hated the cold, though. I can't say that enough times.

I still want to go home, but I know it would be impossible even if I had the coin. My ancestors are calling for me, like to most of us here. Not my father, of course, because I killed him. It was justified, but imperial decree does not see it that way. Patricide is the worst crime that can be committed, especially by the insane. And I was certified insane.

Dismemberment faces me if I were to step foot back in Zhoushan again. Fortunately, many corrupt Chinese officials had been available to be bribed themselves, in order to bribe the crew of an East Indiaman in the port. In a week I had set sail. Never to return – unless I could.

Anyway, getting coin has to be the first step out of here and opium is the best trade for that in London. I'll worry about imperial decrees when I have to. And now Zhang Chen is dead, there is a gap to fill. Another killing to be made.

Everyone wants opium either as a recreational habit, a pain reliever, or for dangerous misuse. I just regard it as a ticket home. Never had time for it myself. Smoking it in a pipe – which we call a *Yen Tsiang* – was only for the weak and troubled.

All of us East India people were called Lascars, and our networks ran deep from Shanghai to Bengal. Zhang Chen had the best I knew of, though. But, let me savour it again, the man is dead.

The key to unlocking the door of unlimited access to poppy was in the hands of a handful of people controlled by John Anthony and his assistant, Abraham Gole. Many would be shocked at knowing what they did behind the walls of King David's as managers. But they were driven by pure greed. Just think of the land and properties they were said to own, if you are still unsure.

John Anthony had other secrets, though, and I knew them, just like Zhang Chen knew them.

They were buried in the Qing dynasty, where politics meant treachery and Shi Hao, as he had been known, was treacherous. First with the Emperor's father and then with the Emperor's son. All for profit.

The five punishments still await Shi Hao, wherever he has disappeared to.

It was surprisingly easy to inherit the opium network. John Anthony was smart. He realised that without a leader from our side there would be chaos. I would never trust him, though.

In London, there was obviously demand for the poppy. But I was sure that more, much more, could be shifted with more forceful, persuasive ideas. I believed it should become as normal to buy and taste the joy plant as it is to eat a potato or a carrot.

Then I met Mr Boats.

Charley Bates:
Dipper

Jack and me have been spending a lot of time together recently, mainly because Dad needs me less at the wherry. Now he rents it out as he's got "other eels to fry", he says. Lil doesn't seem to miss me much, either. I know she loves me, but she's not my mother.

All of which means I spend most of my time over in Fagin's at Saffron Hill. It's funny how a dump can soon become home. It's not because of the place. It's about me and the Dodge. Like brothers, I suppose, but I wouldn't know being a one and only.

I have a good time with him, though, and we've even got drunk together. I don't remember much about it all, but it was more fun than I can ever remember having.

Actually, the whole time with Dodge was fun. Leather Lane was still our favourite spot. And we had contests to see who made Fagin the happiest. He normally won, of course, but there were days I surprised him. Then he would sulk.

It wasn't all fun at the cesspit. Especially when Fagin had to entertain this man called Sikes. Bill was a hard man with hard ways. Never afraid to use his fists and cudgel. I kept my head down when he visited, and I doubt if he ever knew my name.

Only seemed to be two things he did like: his dog, Bullseye, and a girl called Nancy. She was quite old but not near as old as Bill. Men seemed to like her, though, and I knew why. Most nights she'd be at The One Tun singing and drinking and laughing.

I asked Jack once what he thought of her. He said, "Not as pretty as the wherry boy." I was beginning to hope he really thought that.

I wasn't always in Jack's company. Sometimes Bill would send him somewhere for some reason, maybe to look over a crib. And today he was out and about. But he didn't come back alone this time. He was strangely polite when he came in the door with a young boy. Oliver, he called him. 'The innocent one', I called him. Fair hair. Really frail. Angel smile. I should have known what he was as I read big-head in his little baby-blue eyes.

Jack and I had been long-time regulars down the Lane because never once did we set off an alarm with the customers. Nobody knew they had been picked until well after we had moved on.

So maybe we had got a bit too cocky and probably should not have spread ourselves to Clerkenwell Green Market just to show off to the new boy. But lots of bookstalls there means lots of fine-dressed ladies and gentlemen. Fine handkerchiefs, too.

Making a long story short: we're doing the dip, but the gentleman turns round at the same time and shouts, "Thief!", or something, while Oliver screams. We run. Oliver runs but the sweet pea is nabbed quick.

I suppose I'll never know if Oliver screamed when he saw what was happening, which caused the gentlemen to turn while the dip was on. Or if it was after. But I know what I think.

Oliver was taken into the magistrate's court but allowed out when the bookseller blamed a lad with a funny hat, who got away scot-free.

Dodger was strange with me after that. Maybe he felt he should have been nabbed, and definitely should not have joined in the chase for Oliver.

"He was comprehended by the Bobbies on my watch, Charley. I owe him."

But none of it was really our fault, I thought.

The sweet angel's story did not end there. It really had only just begun. Although one of my grandad's tall stories about life at sea would have been more believable.

After Oliver's release from court the gentleman, who was called Brownlow, takes him home – probably because of his fluttering eyelashes.

Nancy agrees to go and snoop around the magistrate's office, disguised as Oliver's sister, in order to find out where he's been taken. She finds out and goes there. Out of the blue she runs into the angel when he's out on an errand for Brownlow.

So, with Bill as the muscle, they kidnap him and take him back to the cesspit. Fagin then starts to beat him and

Nancy steps in to stop it.

There is something very wrong in Field Lane if Fagin, evil though he can be, loses control like that. He must be feeling very guilty about something or other.

If the innocent one does come back permanently to the cesspit, even though I'm sure he prefers the more refined life, I might have to spend more time in Wapping well away from him.

John Boats: Respectable Businessman

1833 is going to be a very good year for me, I thought, as I walked up from home towards Stepney. It's not far but it's definitely not my home ground. Lots of people know me, though, from the ferry trips they've had with me 'across the water', as they call it. Better safe than sorry, though, so these days I carry an old-fashioned cudgel. Hidden away but not invisible to those looking for trouble.

Finally, one of Fred's father's contacts from the RAC had come through with someone to tap in the Lascar community. John Anthony, English name but still an oriental type. He worked in King David's, a place where lots of the Yellows were now put up into as a herd.

I didn't fancy it much. Don't like their smells or their spitting. We all spit, but not from the guts like these fuckers do.

But I had to do it now because after a couple of years making mixtures in his shop, my apothecary had got somewhere at last, he told me. And he couldn't go further until he got hold of more poppy sap.

I always thought the Lascars were a bit low class, either fighting or whoring. Rough. Not diamonds. John Anthony was evidently something different. A bit more noble. More class. Felt rich. Must be quite a bit due to being from a wealthy family and also from his crooked activities. Smarmy bastard altogether.

"The Duke of Cumberland speaks warmly of your partner's father, William Sykes. Especially for the creams and special ointments he provided to his lady wife. In other words, it's a pleasure to meet you, although I assume you are not an apothecary?" He sniffed.

"No, I am simply the close business partner of the son, Frederick."

"Let us first take a tea or a beverage. Please sit."

I returned with, "I'm honoured, sir, but first let me give you a gift of the Sykes' finest unguent: Royal Caribbean Cream Number One."

He did not show he was impressed but I could sense that he was.

A bit different from rowing a boat across the Thames, I thought to myself, looking around the office. Ornate lacquered cabinets all around and large paintings of mountains, rivers and warriors on all the walls. Impressive. But, as Lil tells me, "You could sit on a horse at the Lord Mayor's Show and still not look out of place."

"I understand you are bringing together a new proposal to improve our general health. But it would be cheap enough for everyone to buy and would afford extra benefits with the premium mixtures."

"That's correct, sir. It would eventually be readily available in tea shops, coffee houses, inns, taverns and hotels. Everyone will get a healthier life."

"Of course, it is not up to me to decide whether we can help each other. But I would like you to meet one of my juniors who could make a better assessment." Without a pause to let me speak he called, "Phillip, please take Mr Boat here to the quarters of Xie Qinggao." And then, "I am sure we will meet again. Please convey my thanks to Mr Sykes for his generous gift. Healers hold a special place in the heart and soul of our culture."

The meeting had ended, and I was escorted out more like a pot of dog shit than a respectable businessman.

The Lascar was huge with a pigtail and droopy moustache. Two of me, at least, and I've got Jem Belcher's build. Wouldn't take this bastard on, though, without a couple of others. He smelt of rotten eggs in a heap of street mud but, for a Yellow, he could speak very good English without much of an accent, to my surprise.

The word will have to come up soon enough, I thought, so I simply said, "Opium," with open hands.

He replied, "Coin."

We were off to the fuckin' Epsom races.

Frederick Sykes: Experimentalist

The first year that I spent working with the poppy seeds in order to extend life and happiness for all proved worthless. Boiling white ones or black ones or baking them and then letting them steep in this, that and the other did nothing. I could sense by taste.

Even shaking them in water or lemon juice or honey or alcohol led to a dead end. Nor did shaking them in *sal volatile* appear to produce any sleeping effect or feelings of euphoria, or anything really. That was my last throw of the dice, though, because the salts were always used to revive the discomposed lady, not send her to the arms of Morpheus.

No matter how much I put in a bottle or flask, followed by boiling with coffee grounds or making an infusion with tea or every herb we had in stock, nothing resulted in any sort of effect.

I tested them all on myself, of course. But if I had experienced any effect whatsoever, then I resolved I would have to think seriously about recruiting some young helpers from the streets.

Just after the end of the year my father died from cholera. It had swept the country and was now in London. None of our cures worked, from phosphorous to a quinine mixture with iron. Not even with *chamomilla*. As Father dehydrated more and more no matter how much water he drank, nothing I did was able to reverse his 'blue death'.

The next few months were taken up with my medicinal work at the shop. The only help for the afflicted was really pure water. Adding ingredients like honey or lemon juice had exactly the same effect, but for those 'premium mixtures' I could charge customers more.

I got back to my experiments about mid-year and remembered my father's passing. In his prime I'm sure he could have helped me, but nothing would have tempted me to approach his eccentric friend, Farquhar. Anyway, he had also passed on to another world five years ago.

I had kept away from the poppy milk because it was less available to me as it was not used in foods. We had a source, obviously, because of our under the counter laudanum medicine, but I would need much more for the experiments I wanted to do.

Until Johnny secured more poppy I would steer away from it, even though my instinct told me the pure juice sap would prove to be the answer.

After eighteen months of fruitless endeavour, I had a sit down with a glass of whisky and asked myself whether I should give up. It was late so, to help me think it through, I decided to go to Piccadilly for some entertainment and some more drinking. There was plenty of interest in me from the ladies. *As usual*, I thought, but also as usual I was not in the mood for all that. I just wanted to drink. And I did.

Stumbling along the street home I vomited, and quick as anything a young urchin, I suppose you'd call him, jumped at me and my pocket and pulled my purse out. I was drunk but I was bigger than him, so I kicked back, and he ran. So did I.

I found myself in Albemarle Street, home to my father's old haunt, The Royal Institution.

This place was venerated by those who craved the need for science as much as many people do for music. It had been founded thirty years ago and devoted itself to discourses, public lectures and experiments to encourage the application of science to our everyday life.

It also had a library that could be looked over by members. My father had a card which could be passed on to me if I asked. I would ask.

Next day I visited, and with no question I was given a library card.

The RI is magnificent, the highlight being the theatre with steeply raked seating based on university anatomy theatres. This design allows the whole audience to have a clear view of the lecturer's central demonstration bench. Sitting anywhere in the auditorium made you think you were on stage. What I would not have given to see that old showman Humphry Davy making laughing gas in front of my eyes by heating up some nitrate of ammoniac and getting unsuspecting members of the public to breathe some in, and giggle while acting the fool. I truly feel that Davy's gas should be made freely available to us all on the streets of London, so we become happy and carefree rather than miserable and afraid.

The building was also getting a new façade. Pillars of the Gods is how I'd describe it.

I set to work sitting close to a prepossessing man who introduced himself as Michael Faraday. He said he was working on some ideas for a Christmas lecture he was planning and invited me along. I told him I was looking into chemicals that might help people sleep better at night. He nodded, laughed and said he'd heard many science lectures that'd had the same effect on him.

The idea I had was that poppy milk came from the poppy plant. So, what was in the milk sap? Was it one chemical that took your pain away? Was it another one to send you to sleep? Another to kill you? Or was it just one of many that acted and, depending on amount, led to all of the effects?

Surely these questions had been asked before. But were there answers? Where to start?

Medical and pharmaceutical journals and pamphlets on pain relief or summoning sweet Morpheus seemed as good a place as any to start. There were only a few of them in the library, but it did seem that scientists had thought about this chemistry before. Many of the published letters were written in German, some were in English, but I could read them all.

I started at the earliest point in the collection, around 1800, and struck alchemist's gold. An apothecary's assistant named Sertürner, from Paderborn, had managed to isolate small white crystals from poppy seed milk. Then he put some into food and drink for local rats and stray dogs he had captured. They slept like puppies!

He first published his results in 1805, thirty years ago it would appear. Why wasn't this more widely known? Maybe in Prussia.

Actually, I stumbled across all of the studies because the title of one letter from 1817 was *Über das Morphium als Hauptbestandteil des Opiums*. It had all of my magic key words.

For me, though, I needed to know how he had managed to isolate these potent crystals. And had he ever tested on human subjects to aid sleep, relieve pain, or kill?

It was simple what he did, really. He tried to dissolve opium in various liquids like water and acids and also alkalis like slaked lime. He found that dissolving in the acid solutions gave him crystal precipitates, which he then separated and purified with various washings and filtering. This part of the process would need my greatest attention. But Sertürner was an apothecary and so am I.

The best news was that while suffering from a terrible toothache, he took a small quantity of his morphine salts, as he called them, and got great relief then fell fast asleep. I can only guess at how happy he was to wake up a few hours later.

The white crystals were safe for human consumption. We were on our way thanks to my Piccadilly urchin.

Charles Tanqueray: Clergyman's Son

"I am not amused," said Charles Tanqueray out loud and then thought to himself, *but neither Father nor Grandfather had been amused when I turned my back on the clergy to learn the science of making gin in London over five years ago, first in a small distillery at Trinity Lane and then at Curries in Bloomsbury.*

I was born in 1810, and by the time I was twenty I owned Curries distillery and based it just off Piccadilly, in Vine Street. I had also developed an entirely new production method for England called continuous distillation. Beat that, pater!

Unlike the normal rotgut, Old Tom-type gin, which needed added sugar to mask the taste of the nasty toxics in the spirit, my Tanqueray gin was a distinct cut above. Most people thought me a genius, I know. Others simply wondered if I'd sold my soul to Mephistopheles.

Our product is pitch pure and its flavour enhanced

(not covered up) by the addition of just four botanicals: juniper, angelica root, liquorice and coriander seeds.

"The Beerhouse Act is an abomination," I shouted to my brother, Edward. "Set up by those temperance sops to increase the consumption of common ale at the expense of fine refined spirits like our London Dry."

"All in the name of competition and better health," said Edward.

"Just because there is less alcohol in their piss-water, doesn't make it healthy."

"Language," teased Edward. "You're the genius son of a clergyman, as you keep on telling me!"

I laughed, but it was a serious point as to our future in the business of liquor purveying at the new shop I'd been planning. If there was a rush from gin to beer, then all the investment we'd made to perfect our method and range would be lost.

"We have to sell the idea of quality over quantity and just push the health benefits of including natural botanical ingredients down their throats, so to speak," I told Edward but still wasn't finished. "You know that a lot of this bow-wow mutton is to do with the wishes of good King William in order to improve his popularity with all of his people. Especially the bloody Northerners. It's just like his new Reform Act he'll take credit for, and the Slavery Abolition Bill he says he supports. Well, you fool me not, Billy. I've heard his private views on the Negro, Edward, and they're not wholesome."

"Queen Adelaide likes our London Dry, I hear," said Edward. "Perhaps we can put a special label on a few bottles to make them exclusive and expensive. Call them a Consort edition, maybe. And pass on a few complementary samples to her good self."

"I've taught you a lot, Edward, I see. Try that while I'm searching for some new health-improving ingredients for a Number Ten gin I'm thinking of."

So I went to my club, White's, in St James about a five-minute walk away. It was mercifully quiet at this time. The raucous behaviour at the round card tables under the chandeliers would not start until much later. I took a spot close to the fireplace upstairs in the Coffee Room with its ornate barrel vault ceiling. The French mantel clock there struck three and I settled back. *This place still makes a damned fine hot chocolate*, I thought to myself. And hearing the latest anti-nobility chatter was always amusing to hear. Or occasionally to speak.

I sat down with a steaming cup of luxury in front of me and listened to all the news. Mainly old. Mainly about King William. But some new. Gossip about political matters and corrupt politicians, of which there were many at Westminster, is surely an almost honourable duty for gentlemen to speak of in the privacy of a social club like White's? But it still surprises me to hear self-proclaimed virile males spread tittle-tattle about other men's personal relationships, particularly when stormy waters were brewing. The man sitting in the corner by himself, for example. I had little time for Sir Leicester Dedlock and his loudly expressed opinion that social reform leads directly to social degeneration. But who really cares to hear about the low station of his wife and the rumours of her illegitimate child? Not I, for one. Nonetheless, it was impossible to ignore two distinguished peers of the realm sitting at the next table spreading their mindless muck around. Somewhat more to my taste were their rumours about our pampered royalty.

It appeared somebody had told somebody else that the Duchess of Kent had assured her that her daughter, Victoria, would be the next monarch.

"Come what may. And there will be a proper coronation unlike last year's country show." No wonder King Billy hated her.

Then something about how it was all related to Princess Elizabeth's unfortunate accident years ago after her medicine failed to work. Poor baby.

I could not keep up and instead took a sip of my hot chocolate and thought, *would this go well with our London Dry Gin? Or would it be an abomination? Why have I never thought of this before?*

I snapped out of it and told myself witheringly, *because, Charles, your delicate botanical flavourings would be destroyed by being mixed with a full-in-the-mouth chocolate taste.*

On the other hand, if seeds from the cacao tree were left in a jug of London for a few months, would it add to the experience? What about seeds from the coffee plant?

I need some snuff.

Charley Bates:
Gooseberry

The little angel was always hanging around Jack these days. We hardly did anything together now, which was alright as I had my own jobs to do from Fagin. I think the old bone bag was happy as to how I'd turned out, so I was being sent to a few places a bit away from Leather Lane and the market now to do my business.

It wasn't as much fun by myself, but what really got my goat was seeing the innocent one in the corner with Jack. Fluttering his eyes just like Nancy in the pub and glancing over his shoulder to me with a sort of groaning grin. If you can have that.

He really needs a bit of Bill Sikes' cudgel stuck up him, I thought. *Let me have the honour. Please, sir, can I give him some more?*

I'm ashamed to say that my wish was nearly granted a few weeks later when Oliver was taken out on a special by Bill for a night job.

It went wrong and the poor boy got shot. Sounds cold, I know, but they just left him there. I don't think even I would have left him in a ditch. It was Jack's reaction that got me, though.

"I bet he was putrefied," he said.

Full on tears. I'd never seen him cry before. And then I realised…

It was definitely time to go home to the Boats for quite a long bit. There's no place like Wapping.

We live close to the Old Dock Road. Me, Dad and Lil, as you know. Right next door lives Grandad Jimmy. On the other side is Mary. I'd missed her these past few months because I'd known her since I was five. That means I was almost ten years younger. Big difference but a bit like a big sister. Very big sister, actually.

She still lived alone but had a man calling now, I found out, called Ted.

He'd have his hands full because Mary often helps out on the boat looking after customers. And, like me, she often gets the same attentions. She was better prepared than me, though, and had two very good slapping hands.

The Ferrymen loved her. So do I, I suppose.

A week or so after I got back home, she called round for a tea. She was a big tea drinker and went straight for the kettle that was sat on the range. Lil wasn't in so I said, "Help yourself, my little beauty."

We went back into the front room and sat by the fire. Her on a chair and me on a stool. I took a little sip of my tea… she does make it like a cup of piss, I have to say.

And then she turned and said, "Well, little Charley,

you've got a bit more sauce on you than you had a few months back. Your new friends, I suppose, from the posh parts."

I laughed but didn't say why. Fagin… posh? Do posh people fart all the time?

"Your mum doesn't know I'm telling you this, but I've known you too long not to be straight with you. Johnny is playing away, or worse," she said, giving me a funny look. "Lilian doesn't think so, but I know so. You know he's not home much these days other than to kip down some nights. Straight away I thought, *what's he up to?* And I asked Ted to do a follow or get some knowledge from his friends."

I stood up and pulled my stool even closer to her. "I suppose I'm not surprised," I said. "Dad just can't get off the stage when he's with new people."

Mary nodded with a grin. "But he's not doing any harm to them though, is he?"

My dad was handy with his fists. Not bare-knuckle good, but well up for it. So I hoped he was being a good boy.

Mary just shook her head. "There's nothing that isn't trouble in Cable Street. It's on the way to Limehouse, Charley. We all know what that means. Ted spotted him at The Bricklayers before he went on his way to where all the Chinese hang out close to King David's. So, it might not be a woman then, as he hates anyone who's not home grown. Lil might be right and maybe it's gambling. He's had a bit more coin about him in the last few weeks."

Our place is small, so it only took me a couple of steps to get to the front door. I was angry, and then for the first time in a year or so, I wished my real mum was here. But she never even got the chance to feed me.

I wouldn't have done what I did next even two months ago. But now I knew how to play the streets and alleys. So that night, I went to The Bricklayers to check if Dad was there. He was.

Singing. High kicks. Everything. Never seen him like it before and with a cry of, "Jem", he left and turned his way up Cable Street.

He was an easy follow, even though some of the turnings were a bit naughty. He ended up at a door, not much more welcoming than the one at Field Lane, and went in.

Two things my time with Fagin has taught me is how to go invisible on the streets and also how to keep awake on long lookouts. It's simple, really: hum a tune.

After a couple of hours, Dad came out with a very large Yellow. He was five of me. Dad gave a bow to him. *Odd for him to do that*, I thought, but before my thought ended three more little ones came from both sides, flashed their blades and began slashing at the big one.

Later, I heard he was called a Lascar. It must mean wild man because that would explain what happened next. He pulled out this huge cleaver thing and slashed back like a crazy animal. Dad was on the ground, winded, but then he pulled a cudgel out, just like Bill Sikes' one, and bashed a yellow head in until it was just red and grey.

This was Dad? All I could think was, *what would Lil say?* Then I sicked up. I think you would have done, too.

Johnny Boats:
Butler

'Kin 'ell. "On the floor again but not out, Jem," I said to myself.

So, me being a big businessman means being a thug. Is this really what happens when you follow your instinct to get rich? Making friends. Making enemies. But I'm here now, an assistant to this huge Lascar beast called Xie Qinggao. He calls me Mr Boats in public and his Butler in private. I just take it because I have to in order to keep a steady stream of poppy flowing into our little bit of business in Gower Street.

I have to keep him sweet. Show respect. Keep quiet. You can imagine it churns me up inside. But it's working. Getting jumped like this shows that the number one Kings Fort team are top of the pile.

After our first meeting, Las and I came to a quick arrangement where he would start to supply me opium for not much coin. Then, as long as Fred's new doings worked, we would supply more than our fair share of the trade. Hard bargaining but an honest deal, I think.

Fred tells me he's up and running now, so the next thing I have to do is find some buyers of whatever this stuff is he's made. Anyway, I dragged myself up and saw that the beast had got a couple of deep cuts but could walk.

I simply did not recognise the little pile of rags I saw across the road. Maybe it would have changed things if I had.

I spent the night in my sometimes room in The Bricklayers. Couldn't go home in this state.

Felt more alive in the morning. Shave essential. People to impress. First, I had to go to Fred's to pick up a few sample bottles he had made ready for me. One with his new stuff plus gin, molasses and cherry juice. Another the same but with lemon peel. A third with an arabica coffee bean added. Don't ask me why. Ask the genius.

I had tasted them all myself. Not bad. I did feel a bit dozy afterwards but not floored. Freddy was labelling them as LifeLong. Who wouldn't buy some of that?

But on the other hand, who would buy it? Freddy thought it was worthless hawking around inns and taverns. LifeLong was an elixir for the elite. People who used laudanum for pain medication might buy bottles of his mix if they thought it tasted nice and acted like a glass of wine or two. And brought benefits like happiness, relaxation and good feelings to all.

"That is surely a good recipe for helping you live longer," he said to me. "Maybe much longer."

He was right, of course. That meant gentlemen's clubs and their wives' dinner parties would be our target.

I knew very little about this scene of life. Freddy knew more through his father and suggested Brooks's and White's both in St James as a start. Front of house could be worked by him in due course, whereas I'd try the staff in the bar and kitchens. They probably had a great deal of influence as to what was served to their members. And with the right financial encouragement they might even get enthusiastic.

I was greeted unenthusiastically at the backside door of the White's building where I asked to see the man in charge... obviously using a little coin.

I was taken to a Francis Holladay, who I could tell from the way he stood was ex-Navy. I could almost smell his tattoos. And so it proved. I started by thanking him for seeing me and that I was moving out of my life on boats to a life on solid ground because I needed to look after my children now my poor wife had passed on.

"But it's not just a job I want, sir. Rather, it's an opportunity for you to benefit the health of all your members and patrons."

"I've heard it all before, young man. No need for extra butter. Where did you serve?"

"Well, sir, I come from a long line of merchant seamen. My father used to sail from Bristol with a variety of cargo. His two brothers were pressed and ended up at the bottom during the American War. After that, Dad set me up in the ferry business going to and fro, wherever the money takes me. And may I enquire about you?"

"Purser for four years on HMS *Owen Glendower*. Before that, a cooper. Still miss the fellowship of it all. In any case you read me well, young man, and to be direct I'd like to know what you want of me? Or as you'd say, how can I help you?"

I liked him. This might work.

We had a tasting. Pushed the beneficial effects. Told him there were some newly discovered natural ingredients we imported to make our quality drinks.

"We intend to purvey various LifeLong syrup cordials and we're calling the ones I brought today the Morpheus range."

We shared three bottles.

"Sippers and Gulpers," he said. And did both to each sample.

He began to relax. No longer the standoffish head of dining and beverage at a Tory den of self-importance. But more like a neighbour chatting on the street. Actually, he might well have been one as he was born in the Shadwell area. Never would have known from his accent. It did help us make a bond, although it was the booze mainly. He certainly loosened up with some unbelievable stories about several of the members and, before he dozed off, he said, "That's much better, young man. Let me think about it all. Perhaps you could leave a few more bottles for me to share with my employers. I'll be in touch. And call me Frank, by the way."

Frank Holladay:
Purser

My job was to serve food and drink to the privileged and, thereby, become privy to their gossip. Of course, 'knowledge itself is power', as Francis Bacon wrote all those years ago. It is still true today. Perhaps radicals like those writing for the Independent Whig may be interested in many of the stories I became privy to every day. As long as my name was kept out of it, I would not care. I might sleep better at night, even without the assistance of a bottle of Morpheus.

I was born and raised in Ratcliffe, a small parish set a world apart from the close by but more common East End areas called Shadwell and Limehouse.

Dad was a proud and patriotic man. He loved his wife and he loved me, but he died when I was only ten years old at the exact turn of the century. He was a craftsman, not just a carpenter, and also an active Guildsman of the Worshipful Company of Coopers. That was just as well, because my mother was next to useless without him being by her side. Without the Guild I would have ended up as a beggar on the streets of London, I think. Instead, they gave me an education at their local school and trained me, after a gentle push from the headmaster 'Billy' Robinson, to become a barrel maker.

All these years later it now seems my life was destined to be played out on the seas and oceans just like my namesake, Sir Francis. My only hope, then, was that my lungs would not become as clogged with wood dust as my father's had been.

After school I began my apprenticeship in Chatham Docks. I remember 1816 well because it turned out to be the year without a summer – or the famine year, as we also called it. Was that really a suitable reward from God for the English getting rid of old Boney?

I loved my training and couldn't wait to serve on a ship of war. Until then, I had simply prayed I would not fall victim to typhus like so many others here – "let me die at sea while my ship is in action keeping Great Britain safe from foreigners and radicals."

By 1820, I was a cooper making water and spirit casks on board HMS *Owen Glendower*. Keeping them in good repair was the top priority of my duties, because a leaky rum barrel and a candle do not mix well with gunpowder on a wooden ship. I also helped the purser in securing our provisions and water supplies wherever we were.

The war ship was a 36-gun frigate, which had been launched in 1808 and had captured several prizes in the Napoleonic Wars, when I was sadly only a land-based apprentice.

But I was to see more than my share of action when I joined them as an officer in the West Africa Squadron during 1822. Our job was to help suppress the slave trade by patrolling the waters and seizing foreign slavers. We would then release the captured natives to our station in Freetown on the Gold Coast. We used Ascension Island as a supply depot and it soon became my domain, especially when the purser got yellow fever. No place on Earth could be more different from White's kitchens than the government stores by Turtle Ponds on the island.

In our time we seized Spanish ships, attacked slave castles along the coast and suppressed the Ashanti warriors who were, I suppose, just defending their own territory.

I was promoted to purser on our return journey to Chatham Docks for a refit about two years later. After that we were stationed at the Cape of Good Hope, still fighting the slave trade that had supposedly been banned in England in 1808. I had my doubts that this law was being rigorously enforced, because on more than one occasion we turned a blind eye to the cargo on our own "trading" ships.

By 1830 I thought it was time to take on a less physically and mentally exhausting job. One that was free of fear, attack, imprisonment and the unforgettable sights of abused and half-dead slaves. On the other hand, it would mean I would have to breathe in the foul and pestilent congregation of vapours that passes for the air of London from day to day. Wellington took a shine to me at the interview to become Chief Steward at White's, and I have learnt something about life every day since. Even when I hear the most outrageous claptrap about the lower classes coming from the braying, donkey intellects of the aristocracy.

My nightmares about human trading did not go away with living on land at White's. In some ways it got worse because many of the members were plantation owners who revelled at how the profits from Negroes were still flowing in twenty years after the ban was put in place. If only they could be shackled, beat and made to eat their own shit like their own slaves then maybe their laughter would stop.

II

Temptation

Faust:
Part 1

"To sleep, perchance to dream," said Hamlet. After many months my sleep was finally uninterrupted and dreamless.

It had taken much longer than I had thought to follow Sertürner's footsteps and make the white crystalline solid he called morphine. *Now, at the end of 1833, I could probably do it in my sleep*, I thought. Not quite… but when you knew how, you knew how.

The next step was to work out how much to dissolve. Making laudanum was simple by just putting ten per cent crushed opium powder into alcohol. But morphine would be different. It was the pure form of the popular pain relief we sold. The key was to discover what proportions would cause simply a happy sleepy sensation like half a bottle of brandy. How much of it should be dissolved to make a potent pain killer that did not kill?

As a guess I decided to build up from a 0.1 per cent

solution in gin and get to one per cent. Check the effect and check the taste. And repeat.

I felt distinctly lightheaded and a bit numb at about half a per cent. So less would be better for recreational drinks. I settled for a quarter of a per cent with some molasses or golden caster sugar, with lemon peel in some and a dash of cherry juice in others. The stronger versions could be used to get gentlemen and their ladies to form a habit over time. That would improve our sales.

How to sell them was up to Johnny, but I thought the range could be called Morpheus as purveyed by the LifeLong Company. Maybe Ruby and Gold and Diamond for increasing strengths. And obviously for increasing health benefits.

Then came an invitation I could not refuse… safely.

"Frederick, I would ask you to accompany me to a discourse to be held at the Royal Institution next Friday evening. Your father used to take me when he needed my company for business purposes but, on many occasions, I enjoyed the talks."

"Certainly, Mami. It would be my pleasure, but there will be no extra *fräulein* present for me to entertain as well, I hope?"

"Indeed not, Friedrich. Be there at 7pm sharp and dress well for once. The speaker is a man called Runge, who was a good friend of von Goethe, the playwright of *Faust*. Indeed, the discourse is entitled, *I'm well aware of how much I still have to learn*, as a tribute to him."

"How interesting. I am sure I will have a scintillating evening," I said.

"Oh, I'm sure you will… he's an apothecary," Mother retorted.

The Albemarle building was packed, much to my surprise. Many important and self-important members of society were milling around in polite discourse. The master and wardens of the Worshipful Society of Apothecaries were there. Father's friend from the Linnean Society, Archibald Menzies, was chatting to the Earl of Somerset, a fellow member and current President of the RI. Menzies, who had been apothecary to King William when he was Duke of Clarence over ten years ago, appeared to be slightly drunk to me. The journalist Dickens was also there, talking animatedly to the Catholic agitator MP, Daniel O'Connell – the Liberator – from Ireland. And then along came three people who Mother recognised and pulled me over to meet.

"May I introduce *der Sohn* to you, Nathan?"

"Of course, Hilde. And to you both I introduce my own son, Lionel, and my daughter, Charlotte, just over from Vienna."

The Rothschilds! Rich bankers, all… indeed, more than rich, possibly the richest. Mami must know them through her fundraising work for the German hospital in East London.

Lionel was particularly amusing. We decided to meet in the future to discuss all things alcoholic including a special type he had bought from Prussia he called Danziger Goldwasser.

"Far superior to gin, even the good one made by the Tanqueray brothers standing over there talking to Mad Jack Fuller's Professor of Chemistry, Michael Faraday. No doubt discoursing on the relative merits of naturally fermented alcohol to that made from coal gas. In my humble opinion, London Dry is the nectar of God's alchemy, whereas Faraday's concoction is best left on my apothecary's counter to kill rats."

He provided unstoppable and unrepeatable gossip about many of those in the hall. He clearly did not like the RI President, Somerset.

"The eleventh duke, no less, and descendent of another Edward Seymour, who was beheaded like that other unfortunate Seymour, Jane, later in Tudor times. The man is full to the brim with equal measures of hubris and mathematics. His most recent bee in a bonnet was regarding his name, which he felt should be changed back to St Maur like those of his conquering family coming to England in 1066. What a nonsense." Lionel was especially irreverent about two of King William's three physicians who were in the hall. "Strange to see two medical doctors attending something for which they are not paid. They make up for it, though, with money from good King Billy. They are both much needed, of course, because the sad lot of all Hanoverians is to be born, then die, and go mad in between. Those two know where the bodies are buried and the beds that have been slept in at Windsor Castle."

I could not help but wonder what sordid secrets Sir Andrew Halliday, the dour Scot, and the poor commoner Welshman David Davies were privy to about one of the king's brothers and sister? Especially that brother's sordid activities on one bloody night in Kensington Palace with both his valet and page.

Historically, the discourse speakers are always locked in a room ten minutes before the start, as legend has it a speaker once tried to escape. Let's hope that doesn't happen tonight.

We sat in the theatre and awaited the clock chime signalling the start of the lecture. The door opened…

Interval

The story of Faust goes far past the temptation of Adam and Eve in the Garden of Eden. It is not about innocence, rather, a search for absolute power.

There was a real-life alchemist called Faust, which meant he was a man of beliefs rather than objective science. His character in the play does represent this tension in the human condition and also raises a fundamental question about knowledge.

Obtaining a little of it may be a dangerous thing, but gathering complete knowledge is even more dangerous without the guidance of a moral compass. Many scientists can be tempted…

They are human beings, after all, with normal emotions like greed, arrogance, egotism and jealousy amongst their defining characteristics.

Faust:
Part 2

With no introduction, Friedlieb Ferdinand Runge entered from the door located behind the large semi-circular lectern bench and began speaking.

"In 1819, my friend Johann Wolfgang von Goethe gave me a box of Arabian mocha beans he had obtained from a Greek acquaintance and asked me whether I could extract the chemical compounds they contained.

"The gift was more than enough recompense for a small demonstration I had put on for him to show how the plant *Atropa belladonna* can dilate pupils… and make your eyes sparkle, ladies. I showed him the effect with my own cat.

"Little did I realise that von Goethe's request would push me on a pathway to discover the medicinal and life-changing effects of a pure chemical I call *Kaffebase*, or caffeine.

"The procedure for extraction is relatively simple, as

after crushing the coffee beans the solids can be dispersed in water and later the mixture can be filtered. The white crystalline caffeine remains after the liquid evaporates. I show a sample of it to you here.

"Once isolated, I found that the crystals stimulate the heart such as to give palpitations. It affects respiration, the central nervous system, and is a diuretic. Taking too large quantities can cause nervousness, insomnia and headaches. And can be addictive, as my good friend had suspected."

I heard no more of the lecture. My head was spinning. This pathway was almost identical to the one I had followed to isolate morphine from poppy milk. But Runge's white crystals stimulated our bodies rather than sending them into a relaxation mode.

A Zeus additive rather than a Morpheus.

A whole new range of syrup cordials jumped into my head. I could repeat these experiments and make recreational stimulants for all. Live Long… and Fast, Frederick.

My mother could tell I was distracted and accompanied me to the main hall, whereupon I left her, rudely I suppose, and headed straight for the Rothschild trio.

"Lionel," I said, somewhat over excitedly. "Perhaps we could have our talk about all things alcoholic sooner rather than later. I have a possible business proposition you might find interesting."

JOHN CONROY: ADJUTANT, 1816

I was born in Wales in 1786. My parents were well-to-do, and I was educated as a boy in Dublin just like my parents, who were Irish. My real education, though, was in the Royal Military Academy where I began my lifelong journey in the Army. It was there I became a commissioned officer of the Royal Artillery.

I always knew the best service I could render the Crown was from behind a desk planning the ways of keeping the wheels of the army turning.

Without conceit, I can say our eventual triumph in the Napoleonic Wars was, in no small measure, due to my abilities to provide our brave warriors with ordnance and supplies in the right places at the right times. My most important contribution to our effort was planning the set-up of the field hospital at Mont-Saint-Jean, a crucial piece of the puzzle that is war.

I was well aware of many ranking colleagues regarding

me with disdain, even believing me to be white-livered for being nowhere near the front lines in the Peninsular War. Later, I even heard many reports that I was nowhere near the real battles which ended the war. Maybe not in the thick of it, but I was certainly in the brains of it. In particular, my hospital played a key role in the crucial, bloody encounter during 1815 at the battle of Mont-Saint-Jean, or *La Belle Alliance*, as it was called by our continental partners. I call it Waterloo.

I was cached privately, in case of spies, at Wellington's Headquarters located in The Bodenghien Inn on the *Chaussée de Bruxelles*. The work was gruelling in the build-up to the climax of our over twenty-year war against the French.

The days of 16th, 17th and 18th June were surely much longer than twenty-four hours each. Throughout those three days, my office was filled with important personages and observers for the government and royalty. Also milling around HQ were reporters, artists and, I found later, representatives of various commercial interests, like the Rothschilds.

The most important visitor was undoubtedly the son of the king, Ernest Duke of Cumberland and Teviotdale. A middle-aged man who had likely been handsome in his youth before he received a battle wound to his face, over which he now grew a drooping moustache.

He said time after time that he had been forbidden to go to the front line by the king.

"How will I see my brave boys in the Cumberland Hussars if I am confined to a coaching inn?"

We got on well, though, with a shared appreciation of Tory politics and sharing ideas as to how the Catholic rights agitators could be stopped. I did know that he had a chequered past, being aware of his supposed murder of one of his valets five years ago. And there were more scandals, too. One lurid one involving his sister, Sophia, and another in which he was accused of political interference in a general election, no less. No smoke without fire, I think.

However, he was fiercely intelligent and clearly a calculating man. *Nothing wrong with that*, I thought.

The first day of the engagement is best described as confusion, with all eyes focussed on the retreat from the Quatre Bras crossroads. An important strategic position had been lost. The news sent pandemonium through the whole of HQ. Was the battle already lost? Should I begin to organise for a retreat?

But all was not lost. Napoleon was not coming. Indeed, we won the war on the 18th June. Let the history books ever record that fact.

It was a triumph at La Haye Sainte, except for one division of soldiers who were soon to be branded as cowards: the Duke of Cumberland's Hussars. They notoriously fled the field at about 5pm. It was said the five hundred men had been poorly trained and commanded by Lt. Col. Adolphus von Hacke, who emigrated posthaste to South Africa after his court martial.

It was also later claimed that von Hacke actually had no intention of taking his men into battle. When the request was made for him to support a cavalry charge, he delayed through unnecessary manoeuvring and quickly decided that he and his men had had enough.

His entire regiment began to move to the rear, away from the battle through Brussels, spreading alarm. They finally took up a position about eight miles from the battlefield, in front of the gates of the city.

Cumberland was both inconsolable and in a rage. He was going to dismember von Hacke and feed the parts to his dogs. I can imagine from his increasingly wild-eyed looks that the widespread rumours about his uncontrollable violent behaviour were quite true. I served him my best cognac. Several in fact. And commiserated with him as best I could.

Finally, he said, "Thank you, John. I shall not forget, and when this bloody business is over I shall help you as best I can for what you have done for me on this humiliating day. At least this debacle will make my father and brothers happy, though. Perhaps ecstatic in my disgrace."

Charley Bates:
Orphan

Dad didn't come home for three days. Just as well really, because I still felt sick at even the thought of him.

What would Lil do if she knew he could have killed someone with his cudgel? Maybe he had done so. I just got up from the mud where I was sick and came home.

That's the thing, is it home for me now? Going back to Fagin was not what I wanted. But if my dad was turning into Bill Sikes then I wanted nothing more to do with him.

I still can't understand why Dad had got involved with those Yellows. He hates them normally. And being friendly with that mountain with a meat cleaver? I'd talk with Mary but I'm not sure she could help me. Same with Dad. What could we say? Maybe I need a bit of distance.

But I will want to know why one day.

It would be good to see Jack again. I miss him but I'm still jealous of the way he acted with the not-so-innocent one. I do wonder if he had got back to the cesspit from the ditch. Or if he ended up as fox food? Only one way to find out.

It was actually as if I had not been away for a few months. Jack wasn't in. And Oliver wasn't either. But Florence, Nell, Percy and Kipper were along with a new lot of young ones. They all spoke at once.

My jaw dropped at the telling of the tale. Little blue eyes had worked his magic again. He was taken in by the family he and Sikes tried to rob. Then they nursed him back to life. His fourth family.

The most surprising thing was the coincidence that the gentleman we tried to lift on Oliver's first day of thieving was spotted by Oliver himself getting out of a coach. So, he goes to his house and the gentleman takes him in again! Then the story became impossible to understand, with something about long lost brothers and inheritances.

I'd need to speak to Jack about all of it to make some sense. It wasn't to be.

Fagin comes in. "Bad news for us, the Artful Dodger got caught stealing a silver snuff box and he's in jail. Why was he in Bloomsbury at all? Outside the gin palace? The owner identified him and that was that."

"Caught for stealing a little snuff box. What a crime," I said. "I'll go to the courthouse."

Everyone said no because I was too well-known as Jack's partner on the streets. So, somebody else went. When he got back, he told us what had happened.

Artful to the end, Jack was dragged into the courtroom by a jailer and then begins to lay the law down after yelling and shouting he was innocent.

"I'm an English gentleman, ain't I?" said the Dodger. "I've got privileges due to me. I will not be illiterated from memory. So now you can take me to see the Secretary of State for the Home Affairs. I've got places to go, and I must go now because my time is vocable."

"Who is this before me?" asked the judge. "Has he ever been here before?"

The jailer said, "He ought to have been. I know him well. Everyone knows him."

Jack took a bow and said, "I'm popular, eh?"

Everyone laughed except the jailer and judge.

"Take him away," said the judge. "He has been identified by the unfortunate victim. Off to jail."

They led the Dodger away kicking and screaming.

"You pair of ugly fussocks. I've never heard so much shit from two little lobcocks before. Take me away before I piss all over them."

Everyone in the courtroom laughed out loud.

That's transportation for him, I thought, *I'll never see him again.*

Now Jack was no longer in my life, I decided I'd better find out if my home in Wapping was really and truly my home.

William Sykes:
Fellow of the Linnean Society 1829

Time for a deathbed confession. Well before I am dead, I pray.

It is 1829 and I have started to write my recollections of a life well spent (with blemishes) and will continue to write it until I'm unable to do more.

I am of pure army stock and from a family that was rich. My father was killed in the action in Lexington at the very start of the American Revolutionary War. He never got to see me. As a result, my mother decided to make sure I was trained to cure people rather than kill them in my chosen career. So, I became an apothecary and opened a shop in Gower Street during 1800.

Most of my life was spent in the proximity of Fitzrovia, and that meant Prussian friends. One of them became my wife: Hilde Bannerman, daughter of a physician. I loved her and the boy she brought me a year after we wed.

Hilde changed after she delivered Frederick. For some reason she became much more private and Prussian, often recoiling from my touch.

Elsie walked, rather laid, into my life five years after Frederick was born. Wild Scottish catnip, who I met through a fellow apothecary. Worth every shilling I spent on her for three months of madness. Unfortunately, she too was soon with child. And despite my admonitions, she refused to visit an abortionist.

It cost me dear to keep these sordid matters from Hilde. And I had to consent to the bastard getting my name. Phonetically, at least.

It was the same year I joined the Linnean Society, a discussion group about all matters botanical and zoological. My friend Archibald Menzies and I would also attend some of the Royal Institution discourses in Piccadilly.

It was 1815 when I met a fascinating scientist and engineer there called John Farquhar. Yet another Scot in my life.

But this man was unique in my experience. He dressed like a street beggar yet I found he was worth hundreds of thousands of pounds. He earnt it in Bengal, improving the stability and efficient production of gunpowder for the East India Company and Governor General Cornwallis, no less.

He explained it all to me. And I knew straight away who could benefit from this – the Royal African Company who supplied us with so-called slave-fat that was the basis for our best-selling Royal Caribbean Cream Number

One. They transported much gunpowder from Africa in exchange for slaves needed in the American plantations. And the gunpowder they stored on board occasionally blew up.

I approached them through some of the important customers we sold unguents and herbal medicines to in Sykes & Son. And was duly rewarded for my service of showing them how to keep their gunpowder stable on-board ship.

1815 was also the year I joined White's of St James. Initially to make business contacts but also for the fun and conviviality that comes with alcohol, good food and gambling. I needed the escape because Hilde had somehow found out Frederick had a half-brother. She made her feelings plain by never speaking to me again.

It was also the year of Waterloo and a good many bets were made on the outcome of the various military engagements and performance of the battalions from the different countries. Members also even wagered on who among the aristocracy might outlive whom. There were lots of bets on the Duke of Kent in this regard.

My weakness, however, was whist. It led to my retirement in 1820 and passing the shop on to Frederick.

John Boate Esq

My favourite syrup cordial of Fred's had been his Morpheus Ruby. He'd improved this recipe enormously from his first go by using the pure tasting London Dry Gin made by the Tanqueray's and cherry juice as both a flavouring and colouring.

Two schooner glasses – that is, one of our forty-fluid-ounce bottles – were enough to make you more than mellow and left you without a care in the world.

But now he had made this new drink he called Zeus Gold.

This one had an entirely different effect from our regular Morpheus range. I can only describe it as giving a liquid electric shock. Two schooners of this stuff made me feel like a king. He told me it was basically an extract from coffee beans dissolved in a German alcoholic drink he had come across called vodka.

The first time I tried it, I thought my heart was a drum beating in rhythm to a fast military march. I had experienced nothing like this before, other than my first night with Rose. And I knew straight away that the people who would love this drink the most were the poncy, high-risk gamblers in White's. They lived to be on a cliff edge.

I had grown quite close to Frank Holladay there, who was chief steward. He'd often spout a Shakespeare quote or two and the odd Latin phrase to show me what a good education he had been given, but we shared a similar humour about the highs and lows of life. And a similar anger about the braying and inhumanity of several members, mainly the pricks calling themselves, High Tories.

I was still only able to get a few bottles of our Morpheus range to him each week because we did not have the bottling facilities. Nonetheless, whatever we provided, he sold or drank.

Being me, I soon became itchy to mix with the actual White's members and asked Frank what my best way into their hearts was.

He said, "First, wash your dirty mouth out with some lye. The members don't like to hear f'ing and blinding from common people like you. Then get some calling cards. Then ingratiate yourself to a member or two. You're good at that."

Saucy bar steward, I thought.

So, I got cards made with *John Boate Esq* on the front, and *Health Consultant* underneath. I knew the drill. Anti-Catholic, anti-reform and pro-slavery. To be honest, it wasn't too far from my own beliefs.

Frank introduced me to one of the members standing by the bow window looking up to Piccadilly, who he knew was partial to Morpheus. William Vane, Duke of Cleveland, no less. He was very interested in how Fred had discovered it.

I said, "He is a genius, sir, that's why. And he'd have made his father William Sykes proud."

"I knew him," said the Duke. "The gunpowder man. Member here, but I knew him better from my time with the Royal African Company. He's dead now I hear. Cholera?"

"Yes, indeed. He was a great influence on Frederick."

"Not at the tables I would hope."

Before I could answer, the Duke's son-in-law came over. Richard Arden. Ex-army, Lt Colonel and Peninsular War, of course. He too was a fan of Morpheus, as was his wife Arabella, the Duke's daughter.

"We might have a new range coming out soon called Zeus. It's a real pick-me-up. I think you'll both like it, too," I told him.

"I'll convince Arabella to serve it at our next dinner party."

I'd done just about everything I could today for future sales of LifeLong. What we also needed now was a large amount of cash and a bottle plant. Fred told me he had those in hand and the Lascar was still happy enough to take the earnings from our small sales, although he was always wanting more or goods in kind.

So, I thought I'd go home to Wapping for a bit.

I knew I'd been neglecting Lil. Charley too. But he had new friends now and I was trying my hardest to make his life in future as comfortable as possible by my partnership with Fred.

I got an earful from Lil when I got in the door of our little two-up two-down. From Mary next door, too. They were sharing a tea by the fireplace in the front room, and I thought that it would be thrown over me.

"Look what the cat dragged in, Mary," said Lil.

"Not my cat, Lilian. He only brings home mice. Not rats."

"Nice to fuckin' see you too, Mary. Shame there's not enough room here to swing your manky cat… and then let go," I replied.

"It's not me so much, Johnny. It's Charley. You neglect him," said Lil.

"And we know why. He doesn't call this place home now. Not that you ever made it into a home for him," threw in Mary.

I breathed deep turned round and there was Charley standing in the doorway.

"Didn't recognise you without your cudgel, Dad."

Frank Holladay: Chief Steward

On slave patrol off the Gold Coast, we often saw many large sharks swimming around us. They knew the smell of blood and followed it, dining well when we had to throw dead, sometimes just very sick, black slaves and crewmen overboard. We had no choice. I still have my nightmares about our behaviour. But sometimes I think there are more sharks in White's.

The biggest, in my opinion, is Sir John Gladstone, and close behind comes his son, William. Both MPs, both self-seeking, money-grabbing and immoral. What gets me the most is that all of them are sickeningly dressed in a cloak of morality. Then again, that is High Toryism for you, endlessly promoting the values of the landed gentry, wealthy merchants and the aristocracy – meaning themselves and their friends, of course.

William won his seat in the Commons in 1832 and his maiden speech soon after was an impassioned defence of the rights of West Indian sugar plantation owners. Why that subject, you might ask? The prig probably thought he was being righteous and just rather than truthfully admitting to Parliament that his actions were exclusively connected to his father's ownership of over 2500 slaves.

Despite the Gladstones' interventions, the Slavery Abolition Act was passed the next year, freeing almost one million kidnapped black people. *Gaudē, Gaudē, Gaudē*.

And then the arguments began. The father, son and their cronies insisted on financial compensation. Their reasons were laughable.

"As the government pays soldiers for injury to organs or loss of limbs during war, so too it must provide slave owners aid for cutting them off from their slaves. Because it maims slave owners' economic interests."

So, with the help of the Rothschilds, who arranged a loan to the government of £15 million, compensation was rolled out last year with John Gladstone getting the most of all plantation owners at over £100,000. Criminal corruption, in my view, fed by greedy Jew bankers. Obviously, those who were wronged by their enslavement got nothing. Instead, they became unpaid, 're-educated' apprentices under the terms of the law. And from gossip I lately hear in the club, the poor souls appear to be treated worse than they had been when slaves.

Gladstone Sr, on the other hand, expelled most of the African workers from his estates and imported large numbers of Indians from the sub-continent by giving them false promises about providing them with schools and medical attention. Instead of the promised land, upon arrival they were paid no wages, the repayment of their debts for their travel and upkeep being deemed sufficient. They now work under conditions continuing to resemble slavery in everything except name.

Sharks have nothing on the Gladstones, in my opinion.

"And who will pay the interest on the loan? You, me and our future generations, that's who, Johnny."

These are the sort of people I serve with drinks every day. It's no wonder kids on the streets steal from them. They are just giving out some justice to the real criminals and privileged fools who run our country.

I could keep quiet no longer. It was time for me to add some more truths to the stories still swirling about establishment figures like the venomous Duke of Cumberland. The new friends I had made in the radical world would definitely take an interest.

FRANCIS PLACE, 1835

I was born in a debtor's prison near Drury Lane. My father was its overseer rather than a man who had been detained for an offence. Much later, I became a rather dull and frustrated tailor until I met the radical philosopher and obviously eccentric Jeremy Bentham in my shop. Our bond became strong because of our mutual love of books and the small library I set up in my shop. All were welcome to read, talk, gossip and argue there on any day we were open.

One of my regular visitors was a man who worked at White's with connections and tittle-tattle about people in power. One day he came in with some prime gossip on that dastardly lowlife, the Duke of Cumberland. I had wanted to destroy him for many years.

Bentham had taught me that all men and women have a duty to develop skills in order to right wrongs, no matter what class they have been allocated to by God. Ensuring that justice is finally dealt to Cumberland for a murder he committed requires me to right one of my own past wrongs.

I now feel able to freely admit I took a bribe in order to influence a coroner's trial convened to investigate the suspicious death of the duke's unfortunate valet, Joseph Sellis.

I was ambitious, young and callow back then. It was before I worked with Bentham. No excuses, though. Now finally, twenty-five years later, I believe I have the ammunition in my hand to make good my previous actions without incriminating myself.

A man called Tommy Garth would be my unlikely silver bullet, as handed to me by my anonymous source from White's.

Late at night on 31st May 1810, Cumberland was allegedly awakened by someone attacking him with a sword, who then fled his bedroom. Soon after, Cumberland's Italian valet, Joseph Sellis, was discovered dead in his own room stretched out on the bed, partly undressed, with his throat cut. The coroner's jury, of which I was foreman, concluded that Sellis had died by suicide after trying to assassinate Cumberland in a fit of madness. We suggested a guilty verdict because his frenzied, senseless attack on his employer would be bound to lead him to kill himself.

I know what really happened that night in St James Palace, but I had received a considerable sweetener from the great powers that be to steer the jury away from the truth. The real truth might destabilise the monarchy. Perhaps you can come to your own conclusions.

Sellis was left-handed and the physician who examined his body told us that a left-handed man could not have made the cut apparent across his throat. He concluded the death could not be due to a case of self-murder.

The assassination attempt on the sleeping Cumberland with a sword (by Sellis, the duke said) was inept at best because it was only used to slap not skewer. His other injuries to head and neck were light and superficial in reality, but in the press were blown up to be near fatal.

Several other members of the Royal staff, who all hated the duke for his bullying, violent behaviour, were surprisingly not called as witnesses even though many were at the scene when the dead body was found. But outside the confines of the Palace, many confirmed the rumour (or truth, as most said) that Sellis had discovered Cumberland and his page, Cornelius Neale, on the floor having both Sodom and Gomorrah together. Then Cumberland murdered Sellis to prevent him from talking, lightly wounded himself and afterwards pretended he had been attacked by his valet. Later, he bribed Neale with a substantial pension to disappear permanently.

My job was to muddy the waters with my fellow jurors by theorising that Cumberland had made moves on Sellis's wife, sending him into a rage. Or that Sellis himself was a spurned lover of Neale. Or that it could be simply a case of staff jealousy with the preferment of the Protestant Neale over the Catholic Sellis. My mud proved enough to sow doubt with them.

The outcome I pressed was later questioned by a journalist who published the alternative homosexual murder story in 1813. He was promptly sentenced to fifteen months in prison.

However, the case was still controversial twenty years later with a successful libel suit raised by Cumberland in 1832, the year Bentham died, his body mummified and then put on display.

I am not proud of the part I played in this scandal but now, in 1835, I have been put in touch with an unimpeachable source who is privy to the truth. His given name is Tommy Garth, but he is actually the illegitimate son of Cumberland from his coupling with his own sister, Princess Sophia.

Tommy had been listed as a 'foundling' and christened in Weymouth during 1800. He was initially adopted by a local tailor and his wife, Samuel and Charlotte Sharland. When he was around four, Major General Garth adopted him and brought him to London as his love-child with Princess Sophia. But he was not the father, only taking responsibility for the boy when he was made a Lieutenant General with a promise to be promoted soon to full General.

His death in 1829 profoundly hurt his 'son' because he left the vast majority of the estate to a nephew rather than to him. Until then, Tommy had chosen to make no noise about the rumours he had heard about the true identity of his father. But now he confronted Sophia, who begged him not to face Cumberland's assured anger for fear he would be murdered on the spot with a cut-throat razor.

"Just like he did to that poor valet, Sallis, all those years ago."

At the time the Princess was living at Kensington Palace, close to the Duchess of Kent and young Victoria. And so, she too came under the influence of the handsome Household Comptroller, John Conroy. She begged him to protect her son, Tommy, from Cumberland. In return for being given full rein to her income, Conroy spoke to the boy and convinced him to keep his mouth firmly shut.

He did so until 1835 when Conroy was clearly falling out of favour with the future Queen Victoria. It was also the year he himself became a father to an illegitimate child. On a drunken evening in his club, White's, he repeated the story his mother had told him about Sellis. That information got to me in due course, and I searched him out to see if he would write a suitable article. He said yes. My conscience would be clear soon.

But it was not to be. Lady Astley, the mother of the illegitimate daughter, Georgina, died in suspicious circumstances soon after. And a whispered message was given to Tommy that the same fate would befall his newborn unless he spoke no more about Cumberland and Sellis. He had no alternative but to withdraw his offer to me.

I threw myself into my work by writing a charter for the people with my friend Will Lovett, and in so doing put some balance into our rotting system of privilege and oppression.

Frederick Sykes: The Great

Lionel de Rothschild and I finally managed to get together to discuss my plans for the LifeLong range of syrup cordials.

He had had a very busy and draining 1836 so far, having been admitted to the family partnership just a few weeks before at a family gathering in Frankfurt to celebrate his marriage to his cousin, Charlotte. Then his father Nathan died a few days later and so Lionel became senior partner in the new firm N.M. Rothschild & Sons, which he formed with his three brothers.

He liked the Morpheus range without a doubt and could see who would prefer Zeus: mainly young people. He got straight to the point.

"If I loan you this money, how will you produce your cordials on a very large scale? Where would you sell it? Hawking it around gentlemen's clubs would be a mere bagatelle."

I had my answer. "Lionel, the answer to both your questions is the Tanqueray brothers. They produce the London Dry gin as you probably know. It is one of the key ingredients in the Morpheus range. What's more, they have a bottling facility available. I met them last week to describe my case for cooperation, which they agreed to. As long as I managed to get a large injection of funds from somewhere."

Next stop, Bloomsbury. Charles Tanqueray was an egotist without a doubt. "Good and knew he was good," as Mami says. But he did come up with a new way to make a safe, tasty gin rather than the rotgut Old Tom. He did it by distilling his botanicals into a small quantity of grain spirit. Then he distilled the whole batch once again.

I had resigned myself to telling the two brothers everything about the production of Morpheus and Zeus. But not about the idea of finding concentrations that would prove addictive but not kill. Especially in children.

"Morphine from poppies and caffeine from coffee beans as additives rather than my botanicals as additives," Charles said.

"The Morpheus range actually uses London Dry at the moment. So your botanicals are there," I replied. "The new Zeus line uses the German distilled spirit called vodka, which is identical to your gin without botanicals but with herbs and spices. The big selling point for us is that it has some gold flake in it."

"I think the key to success will be how we sell it and to whom we sell it," said Edward. "I do have some ideas how to sell in the light of the drunken disaster the Beer Act has become. Now that anyone can get a licence to brew, about thirty thousand local beer houses have opened. All attracting prostitutes, criminals and radicals.

"We have to do better, be more exclusive, with our gin, vodka and syrup cordials. So, we should set up drinking spaces with comfortable furnishings and musicians for entertainment, perhaps even food like the fishmonger Pimm is proposing to do with his new oyster house in Cornhill. I hear he's looking at a prime site close to Scrooge and Marley's Counting House by Newman's Court. He will certainly attract all the financiers working in the Bank and also Lloyds Insurance to down his health drink he calls Pimm's Number 1 Cup. Much needed, I think, to minimise the risk from eating a bad oyster or two." He laughed. "Perhaps we should make a counter bid? In that district we would not have the problem of keeping riff and raff out with guards. But the area is quite dead at night and there's no profit in setting up one of our establishments in such a location for selling the type of cordials we serve. So, I suggest we set up our first outlet here in Piccadilly and, when it becomes a must to visit, expand to other locations."

"Good idea," I admitted.

Charles also nodded in agreement and asked if Pimm used Tanqueray gin in his elixir or Old Tom?

"His recipe is a family secret, but we could definitely copy the taste if we wanted to," said Edward. "It only remains to come up with a good name for our drinking spaces and to get Lionel Rothschild to invest," he continued.

"I'd call them Poppies," I suggested. "And I'm sure

Lionel will loan us all we need to do this. He might even want a partnership."

I got home to the shop after dark and poured myself a well-earnt glass of Morpheus. *Great day, Frederick*, I thought.

Then a knock on the door. It was my brother, Bill. I hadn't seen him since Father died a few years back. He'd only come then not to pay respects but to see if anything had been left to him. He wasn't happy with the answer.

What does he want now?

"I thought I'd put a bit of business your way," he said. "I know you deal in remedies and all that oriental medicine, so when a friend came across some old stock, I thought you might be interested."

"What kind of old stock and where does it come from?"

"Some fellow businessmen of mine had a nice set up in Shoreditch a few years back. Got caught but hid away a lot of the goods, it appears. Hid them well and it's only just come to ground."

He then produced three Lucifer match boxes. One with hair. About five different types, one clearly pubic. Another box with what looked like gall stones. And the last with unknown bits of dried flesh.

"Body snatchers?" I asked.

"Yes. Bishop and Williams. Finally got caught selling off the big items to King's College in the Strand. But not before doing a bit of harvesting, it seems. I've got a hundred of these boxes. How much?"

The Chinese might pay a lot for these gruesome items, I thought, *their healers use anything as cures.*

"I'll have to see what I can sell them for, Bill. No guarantees, they might be too old to work. Give me a few days with them all."

He grunted but before he left, I asked him whether he knew any street gangs of young children that might want to help me out with my work. He nodded and was gone. Brothers!

I was sure Johnny could do a deal with the Lascar for the boxes. It would help get us some credit with them for the poppy milk, as we were only just holding our own from the sales to the gentlemen's clubs.

It'll soon be different, I thought, *with both Lionel and the Tanqueray brothers on the deck of our LifeLong board.*

JOHN CONROY: EQUERRY, 1821

Cumberland was certainly a strange man. A mixture of Prussian arrogance and the low morals of the Gypsy. But with me he was, at least, a man of his word by helping to secure my employment with his brother Edward, Duke of Kent. In 1817, I became an equerry.

One year later he approached me in White's. He was, strangely I thought, overjoyed.

"I was glad to be of help to a man with such sound views about the direction this country is going in. I'm sure we can do more together." He took up a more serious and tense pose and went on. "As you know my brother, Kent, is an old man now. Twenty years older than the duchess and without the ample bosom she puts on display for all. Her first husband, Charles, told me she was most enthusiastic."

I was not sure what to say. He appeared visibly excited.

"Perhaps you could provide her with comfort and

company on occasion. I know she would appreciate it. And I would be most grateful, too. Especially if she bore a child, which we could pass off as Edward's. All necessary to ensure what would appear to be a direct succession from my father. I sadly am not able to carry the line."

Employment with a price, I thought. But one I was willing to pay. My wife, Elizabeth, would never know as I would still perform my required marital duties with her.

My career in service to the Royal Family had begun and would carry on for many years after that until the moment the Kents' daughter, Queen Victoria's reign began.

The reasons for my brutal release from service are best understood by revisiting the years between 1817 and 1821, when five Hanoverians died. Three were born and one was stillborn.

The very succession to the throne of England was in a precarious state.

It would have been so simple if King George IV's daughter, Princess Charlotte of Wales, had survived childbirth in 1817. But due to accidents, misfortune and possibly design, the succession turned out to be a game of dice.

The stillborn Prince of the House of Hanover, if he had survived in November 1817, might have become King of England.

The delivery, strangely for such an important person, was not put into the hands of the Princess's personal physician, but rather an accoucheur or male midwife, Sir Richard Croft. His 'medical' training was due to an apothecary.

The birthing was difficult but may have been successful if Charlotte's actual physician-surgeons had been in primary attendance.

The stillborn boy broke both Charlotte's and Leopold, the father's, hearts. To calm their nerves, Croft prescribed a strong laudanum mixture. It resulted in sleep for Leopold, but the weakened mother's body became toxified and she died the next morning.

Sir Richard Croft died by suicide three months later in February 1818.

If he had wanted or been ordered or been paid to eliminate the direct succession line from King George IV, he could not have done it more efficiently.

The battle between the king's brothers for supremacy began. But they were at least now in the game. Although for one the board was about to turn over. Turning mine at the same time.

The Duke of Kent died from pneumonia at the start of 1820, just two years after marrying his duchess, less than a year after his daughter's birth and six days before his father, George III, died. I had provided service to both husband and wife over the last two or three years.

Now I was unemployed as an equerry to a duke but re-employed as the comptroller of the duchess's household. Not an easy job when the Kents were in such debt. I was fiercely loyal to Victoria, a decision I will never regret. And I know she did not either.

Brother Ernest, Duke of Cumberland, I could see now had employed me to make the Kent line illegitimate. Brother Frederick produced no issue. And Brother

William IV's daughter Elizabeth died just twelve weeks after birth in 1821. If only she had survived.

To my surprise, Ernest produced a potential heir, George, in May 1819, just three days after the Kent's daughter, Alexandrina Victoria was born. Obviously, he had lied to me about his inability to carry the line and had simply wanted to humiliate Kent.

Of course, if Adelaide, the Queen Consort, were to fall pregnant before King William died…

III

Knowledge

Charley and John Boate: Child and Father

I shouted at him before the excuses could come out of his mouth.

"Who did you think you was, beating the Chinaman to death with your big stick while he was on the floor? Bill Sikes?"

"How did you know about that? And how have you heard of Bill Sikes?" Dad replied.

I said, "I've been gone for a long time, Dad, while you've been doing the devil knows what. And I've met people. I don't like him, but I've met him and his dog Bullseye."

Dad went white as a sheet. I thought he was going to pass out, but Lil and Mary bought him a stool.

He sat down, silent. And he was never like that. Then he perked up and said, "Listen, all of you, I've got a long story to tell. I've met that big fucker Bill Sikes on a number of occasions in a pub called Union Hall near Leicester

Square. It's owned by an ex-boxer, called Tom Cribb. He's a good man. His claim to fame, if you're interested, is that he beat the shit out of Jem Belcher not once but twice."

Mary said, "But is what Charley told us true? Did you beat a Chinaman to death?"

Lil went red in the face and shouted, "I'm out the door if it's true, Johnny."

"All in good time, doll. Let me tell this in my own way. Bill Sikes is a wild animal and if the stories I've heard about him are true, then Charley could be in danger. Tom told me he was up to his neck in some very dirty business with a man called Monks, who's an upper crust ponce with money. Appears they own rooms in Covent Garden. And rent them out by the hour. From the goings ins and goings outs, it's definitely a brothel. But one with a filthy side to it, because boys and girls about Charley's age and younger are always milling around."

Lil and Mary gasped at the same time and Mary blurted out, "You're not one of them, Charley? Are these your posh new friends?"

"Why would you think that? Any of you?" I threw back. "I do hang around with a gang up west but none of them are posh. All of them are mates, though. One of them the best I've ever had until he was transported because he was a pickpocket. Just like me. But I wasn't caught. I'm slippery like you, Dad. But not as violent. I'm leaving. I don't want to hear any more of your bollocks."

Then Johnny burst into tears.

Lil turned to me and said, "He never could live with you as a loved son after Rose died. He blamed you and was only too glad when you made yourself scarce. But now he needs to make amends with you. Give him a chance, child."

Dad seemed to pull himself together. "Did you work for Sikes in his rooms? I've always known you're a bit light-footed. You never really reacted against the old flowers touching you on the boat. There were times you smiled. Not like Mary here."

"If I'm not like you wanted, I'm sorry, but I won't be sorry about myself because I like me. And I could never beat a man to death, unlike you. But I will say I've never sold myself to Sikes or anyone. And I never will."

All I could think as I left the house was that Nancy would know what was going on and who the mysterious Monks was. I found her at Fagin's, in bed. She'd been hit in the face by Sikes and had come here in case he got even more violent. Nobody else was in so she told me how she first came across Monks, at least his voice. A shout from the street.

"Fagin told me that the visitor won't be more than ten minutes, and goes down to let him in. This odd-looking man with a cloak, silk hat and red birthmark on his neck came in and looked me over like I was a piece of meat and then Fagin takes him to an upstairs room for a chat. So, I slip upstairs and hear what they're talking about. Of all things it was about Oliver. The man wanted him destroyed at any cost because he was his brother. 'A pleasure to do business with you Monks, yet again. Let us hope it will be as successful' – from Fagin."

The innocent one is at the heart of all this? And I'd bet

you my life the business Dad was telling me about with Sikes, Monks and selling young children all had to involve Fagin.

I decided to go back to Wapping to tell them what I'd found out.

I started by telling them about Nancy. Sikes was her pimp and she his woman, when he felt like it. She was a prostitute who had helped several of Fagin's gang from getting a good beating from Bill. I had always avoided his attention and now after seeing her bruises I was worried about Nancy.

"Well then, Dad," I said. "What's your tall story?"

After a couple of minutes thinking, he spoke.

"The old man is forever telling me to get off the boats and into a real business So that's what I've been doing these last few months. Trying to make him proud of me at last. And I've become a businessman selling health drinks."

"Must say I didn't expect that, Dad. Whatever next? A visit to the moon?"

"Listen to this, the three of you. I'm going to make us rich."

We all smiled.

"A friend of mine invented two new cordial drinks. Not any old cordial drinks like you get on a stall in the street. More like magic potions to make you either feel like a powerful king ready to crush an enemy or like a pussycat playing with a ball of wool. But the key is, they help you to live longer. That's why we call them LifeLong.

"And now our plans are all coming together. Soon we will have our own, high-class drinking establishments called Poppies with even higher-class customers all sinking Morpheus and Zeus and Goldwater and Gin Number 10 with whatever leaf or spice or fruit they desire. No undesirable clients, just those with lots of coin."

"What's that got to do with you killing a Yellow, Dad?"

"When you're older, son, you'll understand that sometimes bad things have to happen to make good things happen. The Yellow you saw tried to kill me to stop me and my business partner, Fred, from ever again getting hold of the key ingredient for our drink called Morpheus. Without it there could be no Poppy Bars. No future for our family."

Interval

The gods Zeus and Morpheus only exist in our imaginations. Just like the cordials described in this story.

In reality, commercial drinks like them, giving the same 'highs' and 'lows', became commonplace many years after the events that are described here.

French wine coca is a cocktail mixture of cocaethylene (cocaine harvested from coca leaves dissolved in alcohol), sweetened Bordeaux wine and brandy. The drink was first sold to the public as a health-improving tonic in 1863 after Angelo Mariani, a chemist from Corsica, mixed the ingredients together and labelled the result *Vin Mariani*. Pope Leo XIII must have enjoyed its stimulating effect because he awarded him a gold medal.

Frederick Sykes could have sold it legally, too, over his counter. It would have cost customers about three or four shillings for a bottle… about the same as the price of a schooner of Zeus.

Vin Mariani was sold as a cure for dyspepsia, constipation and impotence, amongst other common ailments.

But for many people living today, it is the inspiration the drink provided for Dr John Stith Pemberton in the USA that warrants the Papal gold medal. Pemberton first sold his own version of *Vin Mariani* (calling it his French Wine Coca) in the early 1880s. A few years later, after pressure from the temperance movement, he developed a non-alcoholic version he called Coca Cola. The rest is history.

In the 20th century, as the addictive effects of coca became more widely recognised, these types of 'health' drink were rebranded as the more social 'energy' suite of drinks.

Krating Daeng was first made in 1975. It contains caffeine, water, cane sugar, taurine, inositol and various B vitamins. The literal translation from Thai to English of the name *Krating Daeng* is… red bull.

And that inspired the formulation of the copycat energy drink we know as Red Bull. Both versions, Thai and European, make anyone who drinks them feel like Zeus.

Johnny Boate Esq would have been very jealous to know that in 2022 almost twelve billion cans of *Red Bull* were sold. And now there is double-strength *Prime*.

Without doubt, he also would have opened a Kava bar. These drinking establishments are now increasingly to be found throughout the world. They serve a Morpheus-type beverage that is not morphine-based.

The drink is neither alcoholic nor hallucinogenic, but does act with a relaxant or sedative effect. It reduces anxiety, increases feelings of wellbeing and causes sleepiness.

One of the first westerners to try it was Captain James Cook when he visited Tonga in the South Pacific during 1777. The tea he was offered was made from the stumps and roots of a plant hitherto unknown to him or his naturalist companion. He described the drink as being "intoxicating pepper". We now call the active biochemical ingredients found in Kava, kavalactones, which are naturally psychoactive drugs. Pharmaceutical chemists and pharmacologists do not know for sure if Kava, like the opioids, is addictive or not. We shall no doubt find out in due course.

JOHN AND CHARLEY BATES: FATHER AND SON

I decided I should leave them to chat between themselves and go for a drink or two at Union Hall to talk about the world of bare-knuckle. First, I had to pull myself together, though, because the shock of my lad knowing Bill Sikes and not only being a thief himself, but also possibly a body for sale had knocked me off my feet. *Rose*, I thought, *would have killed me if she had known what my neglect of Charley had done to him. A poor excuse for a father, I know.*

I went to the bar to talk with Tom, who served me my usual while chatting to the man he called Monks. Not the best looking with a dark red mark on his left jaw. A bit wild-eyed too. But striking in his cloak. Not interested in boxing but was fascinated to hear about LifeLong. Especially Zeus and its power to make you lose all fear.

"Have a bottle," I said. I always carry a couple around with me. "We're looking for potential partners and you appear a clever sort, so maybe we could talk further."

I really just wanted to find out more about him. And I did. His name was Edward. But called Monks by his mother because he preferred his solitude when young, making no friends. Financially independent because of her, too. He said that now he had many outside interests, including helping the homeless and working with parishes to improve the young unfortunates finding themselves in the workhouse.

Then Sikes came in and peeled Monks away. Before they left, I asked Tom whether he was such a fucking angel as he made out.

"No." He laughed. "He owns saloons putting on various entertainments to those with money, especially in Southwark."

Then they left and I followed.

They walked to Russell Street, which is just ten minutes away. And stopped outside a derelict looking building that might have been a coffee house in its day.

They went in and I went home to see my son and beg his forgiveness for all I hadn't done for him. I loved him and he didn't love me anymore, and I will do anything to change that.

WILLIAM SYKES:
DEBTOR, 1831

I was an unlucky gambler. When coupled with poor skills and a tendency to drink excessively while at the tables, the outcomes proved disastrous.

I was in debt to that fishwife, William Crockford, to the merry tune of £2000, my annual income from the shop and my retainer from the Royal African Company.

Whist was my weakness and my downfall. I had been given three months to repay Crockford or face the consequences in Marshalsea with the Mollys and seditionists. I would be dead in a week there, either from dysentery, typhus or scurvy. If not that, then from living in the purgatory of a shared cell with tens of other debtors, violent low lives, rats and excrement. It would not be right. After all, I'm an educated man of distinction with a deserved place in high society as a trained healer. There was no alternative for me. Either I would need to get money now to pay my debts, or later to bribe the wardens.

Now was preferable, especially as I would then avoid my certain humiliation with Hilde and her Prussians. It would be more than I could bear.

Members of White's would tend to look down from my face to the ground when I passed by going up or down the grand staircase in the weeks before Christmas 1820. Not all, though, and I was most gratified that the Duke of Cumberland had not cut me.

"William," he said. "I hear you have had the most dreadful luck at the tables recently. Still, I'm sure you will bounce back. Although, if you don't then please feel free to approach. There are bound to be services you could provide the Crown with your talents."

I was unclear as to what service I could possibly render unto Caesar. I replied how happy I would be to help him however I could.

He thanked me and began with a story he had heard from Ernst zu Münster, who is Head of the German Chancery here in London. He had been in Hanover recently and had spoken to the poet von Goethe. He told him about a miracle plant cure for respiratory problems called *Atropa belladonna*.

"Is it indeed so?" he asked.

"Actually, it is, although too little administered would not work and too much would kill. It is a last resort."

"It may be of use to the Clarences' new baby then?"

I had not heard this news. Indeed, I had thought for once Princess Adelaide had given birth to a relatively healthy child.

"Your paid service to the Crown and myself then,

William, could be this. Should her condition get worse, you might advise your friend Menzies, the Clarences' apothecary, that all could be cured with this belladonna."

Archibald Menzies was certainly my friend and fellow of the Linnean Society. But what was Cumberland really saying? Should I facilitate the new Princess Elizabeth to the other side? Or help her in this?

One thing was obvious: with Elizabeth gone then brother Ernest would be one step closer to the throne when the time came.

In the new year I spoke to Menzies about his views on belladonna. He agreed that with careful use it could prove lifesaving.

In early March he came to me and said baby Elizabeth had become congested and asked if I could make an appropriate solution of belladonna. I did so and, to my shame, made a potion I felt might end her suffering forever.

"Nobody is to blame, William. We did what we could," said Menzies later.

I knew different and was £2000 richer. No longer in debt but I felt I could no longer be an apothecary, and I gave the Gower Street shop to Frederick.

FREDERICK SYKES: SON OF THE FATHER

1837, the year I mixed with royalty. The year I discovered what love meant and met a person who I could love.

The LifeLong products were now distributed throughout London thanks to the large financial investment made by N.M. Rothschild's bank. We could provide for gentlemen's clubs, the dinner parties put on by the wives of members and also our fledgling high-class outlet we called Poppies. We also served bespoke personal requests.

The most important of these was from the Queen Consort, Adelaide, who had been most impressed with the Tanqueray Special Consort Edition London Gin that brother Edward had supplied her with for a year or so now.

She was a highly anxious woman with much heartache in her life. Especially because she had never brought a grown child into the family. Edward had mentioned our Morpheus range when her equerry told him she was having trouble sleeping.

I was summoned to her presence on several occasions as she was most impressed by my German language skills. We talked about how the LifeLong range was developed and how I wanted to conquer the world with it. And we talked about von Goethe, of course, and Beethoven. She described the pain she felt, and I assured her Morpheus and special variations thereof would help her and the king, too.

She said, "He probably needs a schooner of Zeus more."

I laughed and began to feel that I understood what love meant. She most certainly loved her William.

At one meeting, when somewhat over-indulged with Morpheus, she began speaking more to herself than me.

"It will teach the Cumberland sausage right when he hears I am pregnant again. Even if it's not true and just a rumour I have allowed to be spread. It will indeed cause his calculations to take the throne to become worthless. He will throw one of his famous tantrums."

And then she said she would introduce me to the Duchess of Kent because she felt she could benefit from our syrup cordials.

King Billy was indeed a lucky man to have won her.

Johnny and I still wanted to test the strengths and safety levels of our cordials on those who did not have pre-existing addictions to anything. We both knew our ideas meant children. And although he had been very enthusiastic about the idea last year, he was only lukewarm now. I resolved to ask him why.

He came to the shop and told me a horrific story about

ten-year-old prostitutes being herded up in a gang to both steal and perform unspeakable acts of sex.

I asked him how he knew about this and he said, "Because I think my boy Charley is fucking involved."

Worse was to come. He said the organisers were an old lag called Fagin, a strange type called Monks and the well-known thug and robber, Bill Sikes.

"I'm going to stop them," he said. "Will you help?"

How could I hunt for my half-brother? How could I not?

Hester Lushington

Edwin Leeford was a liar and cheat, and I bitterly regret our first meeting at the gathering in London to celebrate victory in the Battle of Waterloo.

My father, Sir Stephen, was MP for Helston in Cornwall and Chairman of the East India Company in the year of Our Lord 1800. His wife, my mother, was born Hester Baldero, and her parents settled a number of manors in Hertfordshire on us as a dowry in 1771.

I say this not to boast but to emphasise that my family were both rich and important. Father was used to having his way, bore many grudges and was ruthless.

My future husband led me to believe he was also rich and important, being a director of Mayer Rothschild's private bank and being given the responsibility to transfer money for paying Wellington's troops in the battles against Napoleon.

We met at the Waterloo celebration ball, which had been put on by the Rothschilds, of course, and was magnificent in every way.

My father and mother were there alongside their children, as well as Lord Wellington and the Earl of Liverpool, the Prime Minister.

I was intoxicated by the power and elegance I felt in the room, and somewhat under the relaxing influence of champagne.

My downfall was to meet the handsome Mr Edwin Leeford. By midnight we had made love twice in the gardens. I had fallen for his well-practised charms and he asked me to marry him. I accepted. I found later that I had also fallen pregnant. We married and in 1816 we had a boy whom we named Edward.

Seven years after our marriage, Edwin had his itch and moved out of our house. Later, I found he had moved in with a chit of a girl called Agnes. We never spoke again.

From friends I found out my husband went to Rome in 1825 and died there. But not before fathering a boy who was born a short time later in a poorhouse. He never saw him.

The mother died in childbirth, but I had no sympathy for her. And most certainly none for her little misborn.

My attentions were now fully on young Edward and making sure he understood the extent of his father's betrayal. That betrayal taking living form in the bastard.

The future will be up to Edward as I will pass on soon, I'm afraid to say. At least he will be in good hands because my brother, Charles, has agreed to take him in and promised me he will help him with whatever he might need in future. I can rest easy for my darling boy. My darling Monks.

CHARLEY BATES:
MAN-CHILD

Was Dad's story about the evil business Fagin, Monks and Sikes had set up in Covent Garden true? Despite being a prostitute herself, Nancy would never stand for Nell and Percy being forced to sell themselves to so-called gentlemen. Especially Kipper from Canning Town, who it seemed was put into service when a customer required the special attentions only the Dark Continent could provide. All of them were my friends and were only about eleven years old. Some of the newer faces I had seen were even younger.

To find out for sure if Dad's story was true, I needed to ask the gang if these things were really happening.

At Fagin's I felt sick. They said they had been doing 'extras', as he called it, for some coin. But they had worse news. Bill Sikes had been here but left in an almighty temper. He said he was going to deal with Nancy's betrayals once and for all.

I soon found out he had kept his promise. Nancy was found in Sikes' bolt-hole in Jacob's Island with her head beaten in. *Probably by his cudgel*, I thought. Passers-by raised the alarm because of the screams and Sikes ran away.

Maybe she had confronted him with the sordid story he was part of with the child prostitutes. Stupidly, I thought I should have protected her and kept her safe. But now I needed to seek revenge, or I would crumple in anger and pain. So, I went to Russell Street to try to stop what was going on with the gang.

I knew Covent Garden was a red-light district. At Fagin's there was even an old book called Harris's List giving descriptions of the prostitutes and where to find them. It's got a bit more respectable since the market hall was built a few years back. But put it this way, I don't think Lil would get her shopping there.

I got to Russell Street and knew straight away the house where the business was done. I knew because I saw Kipper outside it with an old gentleman taking him inside. And there were more children being escorted in over the next hour or so.

Then, the rather odd man Nancy had described with a cloak and silk hat went inside.

Kipper eventually came out hobbling, and slowly headed towards Holborn and Leather Lane. Going to give his earnings to Fagin, no doubt. I didn't want to let him know that I knew anything, but most of all I would not want either of us to be embarrassed. Part of me said, *why were you never asked, Charley?* Too smart or too ugly or too old for service, now I was a fifteen-year-old manchild?

I got to Field Lane at just about the moment Fagin came running out in his smelly rags with a bag in his hand and headed towards the Thames. Now this was my patch. He almost certainly had planned a hideout for himself to use in an emergency. Nancy's body had been found after all. Perhaps everyone knew now.

He ran towards St Katherine's Docks of all places. Probably he was going to go across the river to Butler's Wharf. Would it be our boat *Rose* which took him over? There were few wherries crossing at this time of night, so Mary might be the unlucky one to take him.

I ran to Alderman Stairs where the River Police looked out for the nightly trouble there always was from the customers returning from Southwark.

Luckily the constable on duty was Joe, who I knew well. I told him the man who murdered the girl today was on his way down here to the boats. I described Fagin as a living scarecrow and ran away before he could take me in too.

It's funny it should all end for me at the place where it all started: the day I met the Dodger.

Darling Freddy

Queen Adelaide's introduction to the Duchess of Kent changed my life. She lived in Kensington Palace with her daughter, Victoria, and sister-in-law, Princess Sophia. But an ever-present presence in all their lives was John Conroy, the grandly titled Comptroller of the Household. He was good-looking, charming, tall, muscular and imposing.

The Duchess drank both the Morpheus and Zeus products. All of them. But wondered if there were stronger versions available. I could make them, of course, but had only shared glasses of five per cent with Johnny. Higher per centages might prove lethal with palpitations or a coma.

"I need rest and confidence and strength," she said, as King William was becoming increasingly sick, which meant daughter Victoria would ascend soon to the throne as long as Adelaide was not pregnant.

I made some seven per cent syrups up and offered a glass to her on an evening when Conroy was not present. The Zeus made her talkative, almost manic, and she kept repeating that Victoria was actually Johnny's. It had to be because Kent was no longer able to tup for months before the princess was conceived. But nobody believed her or chose not to believe her for fear of a scandal that would bring down the House of Hanover.

If Victoria became Queen, she was sure both her and Conroy would be sent packing. She now hated them both.

"But why so?" I said to her.

She replied that a system she and John had devised over their years here had returned fire on them. According to the Kensington rules, Victoria was only supposed to be in contact with her mother, tutor, and governesses. Her movement was strictly monitored by the duchess and Conroy, and she was not allowed to mingle with children other than Conroy's daughter.

"But why the need for such an oppressive childhood to be imposed on the young girl?"

"To make her weak and entirely dependent upon us," she answered. "How wrong we were. She has a fierce temper. Takes tantrums. Ignores all advice and orders. Sulks. She is certainly the granddaughter of that oaf, Prinny, who became king."

I was taken aback by her outburst. It was best I left her presence, I judged.

I literally ran into Conroy in the entrance hall. He was very perceptive and saw I was agitated.

"Come to my quarters, Frederick, for a restorative," he whispered close to my ear. The hairs on my neck responded.

He was about ten years older than me but looked better and much fitter. His army background, I suppose.

He offered me Irish whiskey, but I brought out some

Zeus Gold. Within an hour we were both sitting together closely.

He touched my ear and whispered again to me, "How strong can you make your cordial, darling Freddy? Would it affect a young girl's heartbeats?"

"Yes, indeed," I replied. "It could even be lethal depending upon her natural constitution."

"Then may I impose on you to make an extra strong cordial for me. Then we could spend more time together when you bring it."

I left with every intention to return to his arms. But events took over.

JOHN BOATE:
THE LIBERATOR

There are times to stand up. *This is one of them, Johnny*, I thought. What if Charley is actually being sold for his looks and young body to sweaty old men? He said he wasn't involved but he now thinks so little of me that I can't help thinking he was just trying to keep me quiet.

Being a successful businessman is all well and good… at least, I thought I was successful… but I need to close this brothel down along with Monks, Sikes and the Jew. Which of the three was the worst I could not tell, but I hope a special place in Hell is reserved for the one who recruited the innocents.

I could not do it by myself, and I would not involve the police. So, I decided to get the Lascar's help to close this bastard thing down, sharpish. Would Fred be of any help? Probably not, but I would ask him anyway.

Recruiting Las was easy by offering enough coin. Three of his so-called Triad would also help justice to be served. Fred's reaction was not what I expected. He said he would come because Bill Sikes was his half-brother. I thought I was unshockable, but this news shook me.

"Come again," I said. "That bulky lump of nightsoil dressed up in a schmutzy velveteen coat, a bent-up brown hat and a dirty Belcher is the brother to my elegant, good-looking and brilliant apothecary?"

The world is indeed strange, as my old man has always told me.

We decided to meet in Russell Street a few days before Midsummer's Eve.

The sights in the brothel were beyond sickening. I saw young boys and girls being abused all over by fat, ugly savages, who outside the door would describe themselves as gentlemen. *Castration would be too good for them*, I thought. Swift, violent justice was served with cudgel and knife. The Lascars made short work of the lowlife, smashed the place to pieces, yet were remarkably kind to all of the innocent children.

Monks was there, too. I told Las to take him outside.

"Then cut his fuckin' balls off and make his fuckin' face even uglier by stamping on it."

I was disappointed that neither Sikes nor the Jew were there, but relieved my Charley was elsewhere, safe.

Fred was in tears. This was his brother's doing? He wished him dead. I wished him dead, too.

Our wishes were soon granted as Sikes, being chased by the police for brutally killing a young doxy, hanged himself in a bizarre rooftop accident. But there could have been no other outcome for him. God would surely have seen to that.

The man called Fagin was nabbed by the River Police close to where the *Rose* was moored. He'll be hanged, without a doubt.

I went to our house to tell Lil and Charley about what had happened, but neither were there. I realised how much I missed the routine of my old, simple life on the wherry boats. But I knew I couldn't go back to being a boatman, so I decided to make one final trip on the *Rose* before I sold it to Mary. For memories' sake I invited Fred and Las, who had both changed my life in different ways, to come celebrate rough justice on the Thames.

We met at the steps, and I took the oars. On board, we laughed and drank the whole range of LifeLong. Then the bells rang out over London. We must have a new Monarch. King Billy was dead.

I stood out of respect. As did the other two. Then the Lascar's cleaver appeared from nowhere and slit Fred's throat. My last thought ever was, *what will happen to Charley?*

Jian Hai

Xie Qinggao was dead. Jian Hai has taken his place. And now he was on board the *Porcher*, an East Indiaman going from the London Docks to Guangzhou. She will probably end up in the Imperial Chinese Navy of the Great Qing. The more important question was, where was I going to end up? Opium dealer? Warrior? Dismembered? Maybe all three.

Las also died that fateful June night on a wherry on the Thames. It was the day Princess Victoria became Queen. I missed being Las, a good friend to Johnny. We had many great times together and much opium for coin was exchanged between our hands. But I killed him with my *caidao* and his partner Fred, too.

When I was throwing them overboard with the dead rats and dogs floating by, I said a death prayer for them both. But I could shed no tears.

Why did it happen? You can probably guess that, as I'm on a ship to China with a new identity. It doesn't guarantee my safety for my crime of patricide, but it is the best chance I have of not being dismembered.

Monks deserved to die. He was an evil man, but his grandfather was Chairman of the Board of the East India Company, he said to me. Of course, I did not believe him, so I kept kicking while he was in the mud behind his children's brothel. Then I got my cleaver out. He screamed and said he was rich and could reward me handsomely, as well as getting me a ticket home. And whatever else I needed.

"Give me two days," he said, "and I will supply you with money and a ship booking."

I told him that was not enough. I needed a new identity.

He agreed to deliver everything to me in two days. But he wanted revenge on Johnny for destroying his business. *Sordid business*, I thought. But I needed my new identity more than I needed my butler.

I gave him his forty-eight hours to deliver, under threat of the nastiest of deaths I could administer with opium and knife. To my surprise, his family connections worked and three months later I was now Jian Hui on a ship going back home.

Johnny was the price I was willing to pay, and Fred was cursed with unfortunate yin.

But rest assured, if ever I were to meet Monks again, I would kill him. Perhaps I should have done so in London after I got my ticket home.

Charles Tanqueray: Thief

I was a fraud, and I knew it. Many people thought I was some kind of genius for learning how to make gin at sixteen years of age and then going on to own a successful distillery by the time I was twenty.

It was all due to our production of London Dry Gin, a far more pleasant and safe spirit than all the other offerings available in England at that time.

Actually, none of the improvements were my ideas. I stole them from the first place I worked in London as an apprentice distiller to Richard Blunt. He had returned from a partnership in Cork at the Watercourse Distillery, where they had developed a product in the early 1790s called Cork Dry Gin. The recipe was transcribed by his apprentice there and he brought it back to London with him when the partnership broke up.

It was not the only thing he brought home with him. He also had an unpatented design plan made by an Irish excise officer called Aeneas Coffey, a man well used to observing whiskey stills at work. He described modifications to existing column still designs, so as to allow a greater portion of the vapours to continuously recirculate into the still instead of moving into the receiver with the spirit.

The result was not only a more efficient process, producing a lighter, more pure spirit, but also one with a higher alcohol content.

Blunt had died in 1822 but left his papers to his Trinity Lane Distillery, where they had gone unread until I joined in 1826.

I knew what to do, and by the time I had bought out Curries in 1830 the continuous still was a full patent with complete information available on how to make one. The recipe written by the apprentice Caldwell also described the exact proportions of botanicals that went into making Cork Dry Gin.

Tanqueray's London Dry Gin followed soon after.

Now that the company is highly successful, and we are moving into new areas like syrup cordials and high-end drinking establishments, I think more about what I should give in return for my good fortune. It is obviously the cleric in me that is speaking.

That cleric in me spoke more loudly after a nasty incident in Piccadilly just as our sales of Morpheus and Zeus were beginning to soar. My snuff box was grabbed from my pocket by a dirty little boy, but he was caught before he could get away.

He screamed, shouted and cursed all the way to the

courtroom, where I was happy to identify him as the thief. *It's transportation for you my boy*, I thought.

And then I remembered I was a thief, too. Cork Dry Gin had become London Dry Gin.

As my father had said to me many times when I was a boy, "Thou shalt love thy neighbour as thyself."

I approached the judge, told him who I was again and that my father was the Rev Edward Tanqueray, Vicar of Ridgmont, near Bedford, and that he had set up a shelter there for people just like this young fellow, Jack. In return for working the land, charitable deeds and religious instruction, they get a bed and food. Could some leniency be shown him? If so, I would personally guarantee his future good behaviour alongside my father.

The judge agreed. I hoped the jackanapes would, too. Perhaps when he came of age, I would employ him in our business.

THE LIFE OF CHARLEY: MAN, 1845

I can never get over the peace and quiet that greets you in the great open air. So different from the soot-filled choke I had lived with in London.

I ended up at the Althorp estate in Northamptonshire because Mary's parents had been born here, in Great Brington.

I worked my way up until, now, I'm head grazier of the farm owned by the third Earl Spencer, or Viscount Althorp as everybody calls him.

It wasn't just because Mary had told me to go here – because I had lived through a terrible, dark year where my friend Nancy was beaten to death, my best friend was transported and my dad went missing. Despite those sorry events, I still find I like change. How do you know whether the next field is better for grazing unless you walk over there?

I still say Dad was only missing, even though lots of

blood was found on the *Rose* the night we got a new queen, Victoria. Mary still leases the boat and sends me regular amounts of money from profits. But I also get sent large quantities of money from a company called LifeLong. So, I am quite well off, but I'd never find any sort of peace of mind unless I was here doing my daily rounds with the sheep on the farm.

Sitting under my favourite tree, I realised how happy I was because my life was simple – meaning, normal. I was courting a girl called Nell, who lived in Little Brington, and we were both considering, I think, what a future might bring to us.

For the first few years I lived at Althorp I had nightmares about Fagin and Bill Sikes as well as the child prostitutes, some of who I knew. I felt sick at the thought. And now, I think I will stay here in Althorp forever and a day.

Suddenly from behind me I heard a shout of, "Hello, my dear."

I turned and saw a face I never expected to see again stood in front of me. Dodge!

Next to him was a strapping blond-haired lad with piercing blue eyes and a winning smile.

"Oliver?" I said with a gasp.

"The one and only," he replied.

But it was Jack I really only had eyes for. I never thought people came back from Australia. I didn't know where to start.

And before I could, of course, he had something – actually lots – to say about himself.

"First of all, Charley, I was never transported. Believe it or not, my life became a sort of copy of Oliver's. The silver snuff box I stole and was caught for belonged to a man called Tanqueray, who makes gin for a living, and owned a big, successful distillery in Bloomsbury. For reasons he still has never told me, he took pity on me. I think he liked my fighting spirit and cheek, but it doesn't matter because he offered me the chance to repent and improve in his father's parish in Ridgmont. That's in Bedfordshire, about thirty miles from here.

"He ran a shelter for unfortunate people like me, and he said he would try to give me a chance to become honest through hard work and charitable acts.

"I took the chance and lived with him until a few months ago, when Charles called me down to London. He said he was impressed with the man I had become, and especially so since I was now running the shelter so ably. He said he wanted me to come back to London to manage one of his new retail outlets he called Poppies. I jumped at the chance to get back to the Old Smoke, and now I've finally tracked you down. Oliver was much easier to find because he's become such an important nob, haven't you, Ollie?"

Oliver spoke differently from how he had done ten years ago. It used to be like how people talk round here in Northamptonshire. In those days he was definitely not posh. Now he was. Proper schooling, I suppose.

"Get on with it, Jack. Everything is not always about you. Tell Charley about Monks," said the innocent one.

IV

Guilt

CHARLES FIELD: 1852

Charles Dickens is a bloody bugger. Excuse my profanity, but he is. We have known each other for some years, but now I find he has made me infamous as an Inspector Bucket in his latest serialisation, *Bleak House*. I wonder if I get my man or woman by the end of the book?

More importantly to me is, why was I granted this double-edged honour? I live a quiet life in Brompton with my wife, Jane, and am happy in my latest career as a private detective after leaving the Met earlier this year. I need no complications in my life; the cases I am given are complicated enough.

I know where it all began: Section R (Greenwich) Division of the Metropolitan Police. I had been promoted recently to Inspector, with responsibilities for Woolwich Dockyards. It was 1838, the year after we were blessed with our Queen Victoria.

I was approached the week before by a friend at The Freemasons Tavern near Covent Garden, where we were both members. My father had been a victualler in Chelsea and membership of St Luke's Lodge was a given for him, and later expected of me.

Charles Tanqueray and I had met there at the Hall in Great Queen Street a few months ago. We got on well and had a shared interest in helping to develop a new forum called the British and Foreign Anti-Slavery Society.

So, when he came to me to describe a serious crime he suspected had taken place on the Thames about a year ago, I was intrigued.

Charles described how two partners in his drinks company had gone missing, and never been found. One was a well-respected apothecary. The other was a businessman whose activities included running a wherry called the *Rose* along the Thames.

"They both disappeared last June, and the wherry was found after Mary Long, the person who was leasing the boat, asked friends on the river to find it. They found it close to a place in your jurisdiction, covered in blood.

"I wonder if you could help solve the mystery, please? The two men were sound and reliable – and in the case of Sykes a real scientific genius, in my opinion. I believe the son of Johnny, the boatman, is well, but he has moved on far from here."

I had only thought of my job up until that point as one of enforcement and prevention. Never detection. So, I said, "I'll try, of course, if you can give me the address of this Mary Long as a necessary starting point."

A week later I made my way to Burr Close in Wapping – or was it Shadwell? I never know if they are the same or different. Mary Long answered the door. Big lady, ash-blackened apron and forearms of a navvy. Probably late twenties and looking worn. I told her who I was and why I was here, expecting to have the door closed in my face, but she invited me in. We went to the back room where there were some pots hanging and a smoking, cast-iron range with a kettle on top. She offered a tea, but I said, "No thanks," and went back into the front room. Lot of damp there on the walls and some mouldy matting on the floor. Not surprised, though, as it's so close to the river. I sat on a wooden chair between the coal fire and a little table. I wondered if anyone else lived here; it was so small. She perched herself on a stool.

"Poor Johnny," she said. "He's dead for sure, but a body has never been found. He had told Lil and me, as well as his boy Charley, that he was going to become very rich with a business he was setting up with a friend called Fred Sykes. But he needed the help of various Chinese from King David's. Charley had actually seen one of them. Huge. Lascar. Violent with a meat cleaver."

I shook my head and thought to myself, *case closed*. But then Mary went on.

"He wasn't the only problem Johnny had though. He stumbled onto a child prostitution ring that had been set up somewhere in Covent Garden. Run by three people who Charley actually knew, called Bill Sikes, Monks and Fagin. Nasty animals. Two of them hanged but Monks disappeared."

So, Bill Sikes, I thought to myself, *that nasty piece of work is long gone, but if he was involved then things are a lot more complicated.*

She soon got tears in her eyes, but she was clearly a strong woman. She begged me to find the Chinese beast and Monks. I stood up and got ready to go. Then she said that Johnny's wife, Lil, had moved on to someone else.

"But she was going to do that anyway as she was fed up to the back teeth with him. Always talking about one big deal or another. Always on the fly, 'til they crashed to the ground."

I started towards the front door and opened it to get some fresh air. I was beginning to feel strangled by the smoke. Then she said Charley was safely away in Northamptonshire at the place where she was born.

"He needed more than a change of scene. He needed a change of life. And I think he's got it now after a few years away from the Smoke."

I thanked her and said I'd let her know of any progress I made in the coming weeks.

Two weeks after that, I managed to find time to go to King David's Fort Barracks near the Shadwell Basin. An introduction took me to the manager, John Anthony. *Urbane but untrustworthy*, I thought.

"Yes, your description fits one of the people who used to live here, Xie Qinggao. One day, over a year ago, he left, he told us, for the Americas. But I know better. He got himself a contact in the East India Company who bought him a ticket on an East Indiaman ship. He also was spending far more money than he ever had before. And somehow got new identity papers without which he would be a dead man in China.

"I would suspect his contact was a rather strange

character who Xie Qinggao began to take to opium houses in Limehouse. The name is Edward Leeford, sometimes called Monks, and his uncle is on the board of the EIC, like his grandfather before him.

"I liked Mr Boate and regret what surely is his passing. Perhaps you would like some refreshment now our interview is concluded?"

I decided against tea and gave a small bow of thanks, as I believe is customary with the Orientals. *Interesting*, I thought, *of some help but not nearly enough. I'd love to know what crooked activities that man is involved in.*

Then I walked to the next obvious port of call for me, the East India Company. An evil that England could do without, in my opinion, especially due to its long-standing connection to slave cargo. Even doing such things now, I believed.

East India House was in Leadenhall Street to the east of the Bank of England, which is the financial centre of the City of London. It was an unsurprisingly grand building with a six-column portico entrance and Britannia sitting on top.

My thoughts were mixed upon entering. Mainly repulsion about what had been done here in the name of profit and power, but also anticipation of clues being revealed as to help identify a trail to find Charles's partners' killers.

I showed my warrant number, 520 – one of the first issued for the Metropolitan Police, I am proud to say – to a uniformed fellow in the grand entrance hall, which was full of oil paintings and sculptures.

He took me to a director's office. This man, whose name I never knew because it was not disclosed, said that no Leeford was or ever had been a director here. Disappointing.

I thought immediately of an Irishman I knew well called William Maginn, who was a contributor to the well-known society and scandal Sunday paper called *The Age*. I had given him information in the past about some of the lurid goings on I had been involved with in my career. Perhaps he might return a favour about the EIC. It was only a thirty-minute walk along the Thames to the Strand, where many of these salacious rags were published. I think it will be worth it.

"Happy to help if I can, Chorles," he said. I never knew why he seemed incapable of saying Charles.

"I'm looking at a murder case involving Edward Leeford. Apparently, he is a grandson of a past chairman of the EIC. I'm looking for him with a view to interview."

"The infamous Waterloo Ball of 1816 at the Royal College of Surgeons is what you are seeking, Chorles. The shame of Hester, a daughter of Sir Stephen Lushington and, as you say, Chairman of the Board in 1800. She was, shall we say, indelicate with a handsome young man in the gardens. He was called Edwin Leeford, and from her coupling she ended up with child.

"Their son Edward is, by all accounts, a strange, disfigured creature, but I have heard nothing about him at all in recent years. He did have a sad life, though. His father left his mother for a loose woman, fathered a boy and soon died himself. Before she died, Hester passed on the responsibility for Edward to her brother, Charles Lushington, who is indeed a director of the EIC."

"Thank you, William. I owe you a bottle of Cork Dry Gin."

It was another week before I got back to Leadenhall Street, but this time I had an appointment with Charles Lushington. *A well-mannered gentleman*, I thought upon entering his spacious room. But a slight nervous tic was apparent.

"Thank you, sir, for agreeing to see me. I'll cut to the chase and ask if you have any knowledge of where your nephew, Edward, may be?"

"Has he committed a crime?" he replied.

I shook my head. "Not as far as I know for sure. When did you last see him? And did he ask for any favours at that time?"

"Please, Inspector, I made a solemn promise to my late sister that I would look after Edward after she died. I confess I did not like him. Selfishness and jealousy ran his life, and I can't imagine him having any concept of the word love.

"In any case, I granted him three wishes when I saw him last year. Final wishes, I told him, I might add. The first was passage for a Lascar he knew to travel to China. The second was to give the Chinaman new identity papers, which are easy to obtain here in the EIC. The third was more unusual. Edward wanted a boat ticket to the Americas. Not Asia, as I would have expected. I got them to him within forty-eight hours, because he impressed on me the urgency for his very survival. And that was that."

"Where did he want his ticket to go to?"

Charles replied, "Liverpool to New Orleans. I did not question him. I just wanted him out of my life."

I soon found out Monks had left Liverpool on 11th February 1838 on the *Aractius* and landed in New Orleans on 29th March.

A very satisfactory piece of detection, I felt. Perhaps I'll do more one day.

Jack Dawkins's Gang

"It's time to tell our stories," I said to the other two. "Is there a place we can get a drink?" I asked Charley.

There was indeed a hostelry nearby called The Althorp, so we walked from the tree we had squatted down at and through the estate, passing the oval lake with its own island and, soon after, Charley's little cottage. It was certainly beautiful, although the quiet life would not have suited me now that I was living back in London.

The stone and thatch inn he took us to was in sight of an ancient church being renovated, called St Mary's. It probably was in need of it, as Charley said it was over five hundred years old.

"You go first," I said to Charley.

And then he began.

"I'll never forgive myself for what I said to Dad the last time we met at the house in Wapping. I couldn't believe he thought I was responsible for my mother's death. And that he didn't love me. I told him I was sorry I couldn't be the son he wanted, but I wasn't sorry about myself being myself, because I like me."

I looked at Oliver and he looked back at me. I bet he's thinking of his own story in the workhouse.

Charley carried on. "Then he spun a sorry story about how Fagin's gang along with Monks and Bill Sikes were running a brothel in Covent Garden using child prostitutes. He asked me if I was on the menu, too. I told him I'd never sold myself to Sikes and I never would. And unlike him I couldn't beat a man to death. Then Dad started to cry like a baby with colic."

Oliver jumped in. "Look, Charley, if this is too upsetting for you then we don't need to know." And he offered a clink of his beer mug with the pair of us. We took it.

"No, really, all's good. Sometimes I imagine telling this story to you two. It makes me feel better. Never thought the day would actually come when we'd be together again. Anyway, I decided to leave the house and went to Field Lane to check on Johnny's story, only to find poor Nancy there on her bed. She had been beaten up by Bill in one of his drunken rages. Then she told me about Monks and Fagin talking about their special business together. So, I turned round again for Wapping to see what Dad had to say for himself, and whether 'special business' meant selling my friends to many and various gentlemen for their pleasure."

Oliver reddened up because he remembered what had happened to him in the undertaker's shop, a lifetime ago.

"When I got back, Johnny told what I thought was another tall story about how one of his friends had invented a drink that would make us all very rich. Lil,

Mary and I were all speechless at hearing this pile. And then he left our house and I never saw him again."

We all looked at each other and realised our drinks had gone down our throats, so I sent Ollie up to the bar for some refills. He came back with a beer and a Scotch each. At least it put a smile back on Charley's face before he went on.

"The next day I went back to Fagin's for the last time and saw Kipper, Flo and Jim there. They told me that the Covent Garden story was true, and they had been sworn to secrecy. For some reason or other, Bill had taken it into his head that Nancy had betrayed him to the police, and he had gone off to deal with her once and for all. And he did, as we all know. But he soon got justice, as did Fagin. That old bag of bones was caught trying to get across the Thames to hide in his bolt-hole. Just like Sikes had done. Thanks be to God that while trying to escape the hue and cry Bill fell from a rooftop and hanged himself. Bullseye the dog, loyal to the end, fell or jumped off alongside his master."

I said, "Right, lads, let's make a toast to that. Unless there's more good news, Charley?"

"Well, yes there is. Fagin later went to trial and was hanged, too. It was too gentle a punishment for that child slaver, I've always thought… and I tell him so whenever I wake up from one of my nightmares about him and Bill and poor Nancy."

"Gentlemen, and I count myself in on that these days, a toast to fitting ends."

We gulped our whiskies back and Oliver got up to get another three.

Charley finished off his story on a happy note, I'm glad to say. He, of all the people I've ever known, is the most trustworthy and loyal. I love him like a brother.

"You know the rest. Lil and Mary sent me to Northamptonshire to get away from it all. That's why we're here now, in Great Brington. And, as you can tell, I couldn't be happier than being with the pair of you again."

"You next, Oliver," I said. "But I need to visit outdoors first." And I did. Quickly.

"I didn't know my mother either, Charley. Like you, she died so I could live. My father, Edwin Leeford, had left her to travel to Rome to secure his own inheritance. But he died there and left my mother to give birth in a workhouse. So, my father never met me.

"I was told the story much later by Mr Brownlow. You remember him? He was the gentleman you tried to steal from in Clerkenwell, but it all went wrong because of me being stupid on my first outing with you two. I still remember it all. I had no idea you were going to pickpocket him. So, I screamed when I saw what you were doing. I'm sorry, gentlemen. Hope you can forgive me."

"Well, Ollie, it might take a few more drinks before we could do that, mate."

Charley nodded and I could see tears in his eyes. Happy tears though.

"Anyway, I lived in the workhouse and on a farm for about ten years. I didn't have a name until old Beadle Bumble came up with Oliver Twist. Then I was given a job in an undertakers, which I hated, but stayed until I was beaten up and worse for standing up to a bully. So, I ran off to London and there I met Jack and you. And, of course, Fagin. Believe it or not, they were some of my happiest times because I felt part of a family at last. That is, until I got shot."

He laughed and so did we. *Nobody could write this in a book*, I thought.

"Then I came across Monks, who was my stepbrother, trying to get me arrested so I would get no inheritance from my real family. Later, Mr Brownlow told me my name was Leeford, and my father had been his best friend. So, gentlemen, may I introduce to you the rich and handsome Oliver Leeford Esq."

Charley and I made sicking up noises, but the truth is that Oliver Twist is now one tall, good-looking and rich gentleman.

"My turn," I said. "I think you'll think it's well worth the wait."

The other two raised their eyebrows. So, I went on.

"My story starts last year when Mr Tanqueray brought me down to Poppies in Piccadilly. It's a high-class drinking establishment, but not a gentleman's club – more relaxed than that. First of all, he showed me a big glass cabinet that was full of bottles. Three shelves of a drink called Morpheus and three of one called Zeus. He said these drinks had helped make the company the financial success it was today. They had been invented by two people. The first was Frederick Sykes, an apothecary, and the second a businessman called John Boate, or sometimes called Johnny Boats."

Charley shot up out of his chair on hearing this, I bet

thinking that his dad hadn't fed him shit after all. He didn't say anything though, so I carried on.

"They were both killed in a wherry called the *Rose* on the Thames a few years ago. Bodies never recovered. No suspects. Until Mr Tanqueray asks a policeman friend to look into it. He found that a large and violent Lascar had killed them both under the instruction of a man called Monks."

Charley and Oliver both fisted the table at the mention of his name. Both had reason to hate Monks now. I carried on but my voice was cracking up.

"I think he's a mad dog needing to be put down, too. He was the one who thought up and set up Fagin's brothel and caused all my gang to be broken to pieces for life. I know because I've spoken to Kipper and Flo and Jim, too. They're eighteen now and still can't sleep at night because of the services they were made to provide.

"I think we must get all the people he tried to destroy, including you, Oliver, some justice. But which of the three of us will do the deed?"

I pointed at Charley. Charley pointed at Oliver, and he pointed at me. We burst out laughing.

"And I know where to start: New Orleans in the United States. It's the first place Monks sailed to. So, are we together on this? We don't need to take an oath and write our names in blood or anything like that, but we can raise a glass. To justice, gentlemen."

"To justice," they both replied, and the three of us linked hands across our shoulders.

"No singing of 'Auld Lang Syne' though, please, gentlemen."

Dr Michael O'Reagan, 1846

I'm standing on the banks of the Mississippi where I can see a hundred ships, both sail and steamboat – the transport driving the beating heart of New Orleans.

It was August 21st, and unlike several other crossings from Liverpool made recently, the ship I had come to meet had not needed to turn back at any point. The *Home* left on July 10th and my brothers, Terence and James, and my sister, Alice, would be on board with news, I hope, of Mother and even Father. They would surely have news about the violence in the streets now. Because of the famine and food shortages, people were suffering. *It can only get worse*, I thought.

I had to leave Dublin in 1842 and take up a job here as a physician because of my father's crimes. *Successfully defending his systematic embezzlement from a charity-funded hospital would have been beyond the powers of even the great Daniel O'Connell*, I thought.

The O'Reagans had been a well-respected family living in Portobello near to St Patrick's Cathedral. Our house was fairly close to the place where Father and I worked, the Cork Street Fever Hospital. We took in patients from all over Dublin, and I treated hundreds of cases of cholera, typhus, yellow fever and scarlet fever in my five years there.

My father was not only a physician but was also in charge of raising and distributing donations and subscriptions. This was a substantial annual sum, but dwarfed by the running costs provided by devout religious philanthropists such as Arthur Guinness.

The hospital itself was constructed as two buildings in order to separate the infectious sick physically from the convalescent patients. The approach proved to be very successful, and our mortality rates dropped remarkably over time.

Arthur Guinness II had much more of an interest in banking and accountancy than his father. Unfortunately for my father. Suspecting his long-term pilfering from the Cork Street accounts would be discovered, he simply disappeared without a word to his colleagues or family.

I could not carry on working there with any level of honour. So, I resigned.

Our family had been left poor, although not destitute, so I resolved to emigrate to a place that needed my medical skills and, more importantly, paid well.

My attention turned to New Orleans because it suffered almost continual epidemics of infectious diseases as well as housing a very poor population. It also had a famous infectious disease hospital called the Charity, with a newly constructed building near Faubourg St Marie in the centre of the American section.

The city could not be more different from Dublin than a dog is from a cat. First of all, the place is hot and humid, almost above the boiling point of any normal Irishman. It is a mixed race, class-ridden and a strangely divided city to live in. For example, streetcar segregation, meaning no Blacks (or 'coloureds', as they are sometimes called) on board, has been practiced as policy by the transport companies from the first mule-drawn trams in the 1820s. I thought it unjust because they were popular and clean, particularly in the hotter seasons, as opposed to the poorly ventilated omnibuses the Negroes were allowed on, albeit begrudgingly. The heart of the problem was that the black population, both free and slave, outnumbered the number of Whites, so troubles were always likely.

I soon got to learn that segregation was a reaction to the minority status of the Whites. But they held the power. Some of the omnibuses excluded black passengers altogether, while others allowed black nurses with white children to get on board. Streetcars marked with a black star were put in place to transport so-called free people of colour and also slaves, to whom the omnibuses were closed. But they were infrequent, usually every third or fourth car; so they were social tinderboxes. The system put Whites in a very public position of superiority so as to separate them from Blacks, or 'the trash', as I sometimes heard them called. As might be expected, such an arrangement caused an ever-present friction with

Blacks resisting this segregation, sometimes violently by confronting drivers.

They were not the only tensions, though, because there are as many social layers here in New Orleans as there are fish in a pot of Antoine's bouillabaisse.

The Creoles, who would describe themselves as the establishment, lived in the French Quarter section. They felt they were superior to those living in the American section, as they were the indigenous population upon which the city had been built.

Both sections had substantial numbers of European immigrants in their street blocks, mainly German, some Scandinavian and some Irish. And like back in England, there could be cruel discrimination directed towards us Irish from even the Creoles.

That's not to say prejudice did not exist in Ireland. There was a Protestant versus Catholic divide. Another between urban and rustic life. Accents made all the difference in social standings. And having money and land too helped a lot.

Despite the stifling heat in New Orleans and the good chances of catching a disease like yellow fever (I did so myself last year when I was nursed by a voodoo queen, believe it or not), I was content here. Even though I was not as motivated by the mighty dollar, as most of my American colleagues were. But I was able to send money home to Mother and invite three of my siblings to come visit me, and perhaps settle down.

I have to say, though, there are things happening here which I could never get used to, let alone condone. The most sickening being the slave trade, something that had stopped years ago in England and Ireland.

New Orleans did not confine its slave trade to one single marketplace or even a handful of them. Instead, slaves were sold citywide in places like the St Louis Hotel, private residences, public parks or decks of ships moored along the Mississippi. I despaired at the high-walled slave pens built near to commercial complexes such as Banks Arcade, which served as one of the locations for buying and selling Negroes on most days. Even the British did not do that at home, much as some of them might have liked to.

I did attend one of these auctions out of curiosity. It was demeaning. Mouths opened to check teeth, genitalia fondled intimately to assess stamina, and physical assessments of general muscularity. The whole thing was a cross between business and entertainment. Buyers could generally purchase a fine male specimen for about $500 – that is, £100. I have no idea if it is a fair price for a human being or not. I would think less of myself if I did.

I could see the *Home* mooring and thought once again upon how the Mississippi ruled this city like a water-filled aorta allowing for commerce to take place with manufactured goods going upstream, and produce like sugar cane and cotton coming downstream.

Soon, two men and a woman approached me. I was overwhelmed and cried. So did they.

I had just about recovered to say, "Welcome to your new home", when three young men, who had been hovering around them, came up and smiled.

One of them said, "Bloody hot here, isn't it? Heard a lot about you, Mick. I'm Jack. And these are my two friends, Oliver and Charley. Pleased to make your acquaintance. Alice said it would be fine."

The Duke of Southwark, 1844

It is time to tell my true story. Finally put to rest those ramblings by the sanctimonious hack Dickens. Making that insipid boy called Oliver into a sympathetic hero. And his mother into a lost soul rather than the slut-hole she was.

My mother was badly wronged by Edwin Leeford, her hurt never recognised other than by me. She loved her man and he simply walked out of her life. No apologies or concerns. No thought for me, his firstborn.

Is it any wonder I have always needed to prove myself in my own way? And to get vengeance for my mother.

Anything is possible with sufficient money, and so being rich has been my dream ever since I left school. I had come from a wealthy family with some considerable standing in society because of its association with the East India Company. The most important benefactor for me, though, was my mother's eldest brother, Sir Henry, who was Consul General to Naples and also my godfather. He provided me with a most generous annual allowance, which gave me the freedom to invest in whatever businesses I felt would be most lucrative.

That holier-than-thou fool Dickens got one thing right: I am a physical coward. But being so has never prevented me from courting danger, at a safe distance, or dealing with the raw underbelly of life.

Fagin was just one of the low-lives I have worked with for my profit. But he was simply a means to an end in my scheme to destroy my half-brother.

My main income comes from my support of, and investment in, a number of night-time entertainments for paying guests and their courtesans in various establishments I had purchased across London.

The Grapes Public House in Mint Street by Southwark Bridge was my first successful venture. The saloon bar I had attached to it put on musical entertainments as well as private theatricals. In fact, it acted as a front of house for a brothel catering for every specialist taste. Later, I called it the Duke of Southwark's Music Hall to give it an air of respectability. It was highly profitable, as many of the non-debtor inmates of nearby Marshalsea Prison, especially those imprisoned by the Admiralty for 'unnatural crimes', would regularly visit. Most of my other patrons came over from the City of London by wherry to Bankside pier. I still hold my memories of The Grapes firmly in my heart as well as my pocket, even though I now live in New Orleans.

Thank God for my mother binding her brother Charles to me for whenever I needed his help. I would be dead now if it were not for him getting me passage to the United States and a ticket to China for the Lascar wild animal.

I thought there would be only a slim chance that the police would follow my route to New Orleans, a highly unlikely destination for most with its yellow fever and cholera outbreaks. But in its favour, I knew the place rolled in money coming from sugar cane and cotton plantations. It also had slaves, dance halls, prostitutes, drunks and criminals.

I spent almost fifty days aboard the *Aractius* to get here from Liverpool. There was hardly a day when I was not sick.

The journey was only made bearable by evening card games with the few other passengers on board. We began with whist as we were mainly English. But that soon got taken over by an exciting game of bluff, which an Irish-American introduced us to, called poker.

Archie Murphy was a big man in every sense. Filled a room with laughter and stories, most of a salacious kind, but many genuinely funny about things that had happened to him in life.

He was brought, at age fifteen, to the United States by his father, who managed an estate in Mitchelstown near Waterford. They exported salt beef, pork, butter and hard cheese through the slaughterhouse, port city of Cork.

During the Napoleonic Wars, exports boomed from supplying England, the Royal Navy and the sugar colonies of the West Indies. The Murphys became very rich. But the end of the war in 1815 meant potential economic disaster. So, the whole family emigrated to the United States.

Archie's father chose for them to go to New Orleans for its uninhibited good times, after living in the repressed Catholic and cruel British client state called Ireland.

And they had never looked back, until Archie decided to pay a visit to what he called the 'decies' a year ago, just to breathe in the air for one final time and say a prayer to his ancestors.

He now worked in the entertainment industry, he said, as the real lifeblood of New Orleans was not sugar or cotton, it was alcohol, gambling, dancing and sex.

I told him I had similar business interests in London, with a number of saloons and music halls in my possession. I then let him know that if he were ever in need of investment for expansion of his empire, then I'd be happy to oblige.

"Let's shake hands on that, Edward," Archie said.

"Maybe having the Duke of Southwark on your letterheads will help attract even more investors for you," I replied.

I finally met Archie on land four months later, but in the meantime, I had been busy trying to sample all the *bon temps* he had talked about.

One place I heard named time after time in all the bars and cabarets I went to in my first week was the Maison Blanche on the shores of Lake Pontchartrain. Especially on St John's Eve – Midsummer's Eve, to the British.

The Maison was a classy bordello run by the New Orleans Queen of Voodoo, I was told. Sounds like a pile of hoodoo from a cow's backside to me, but if the place has got the best drinks and drugs and whores then it also sounds like heaven.

It was only five miles away by train from Faubourg in the city to Milneburg on the Lake, and then a horse-drawn carriage was put on to collect the customers.

The owner was a very impressive mulatto, who dressed all in white. Today wearing a long flowing gown with bustier laces tied across her magnificent diddies. And topped with a turban shaped like a king cobra.

When we met in the greeting room she straight away said, "My name is mamzelle Marie Laveau. I am a free woman of colour. Proud and uncommonly beautiful, I'm told by my clients and their servants. I'm also a Voodooienne."

You couldn't fault her flair for dramatic introductions, I suppose. Or, as I soon found out, the quality of the alcohol and the prostitutes *en Maison*.

My first night there remains with me only as a drugged haze in my mind. Partly due to opium and partly from a chemical milked in front of my face from a puffer fish caught locally. They called it the zombie drug.

Too much could kill, too little only gave a tingling sensation, but the correct amount turned you into what they called an 'undead' – that is, being in a half-world, neither in life nor death.

I accepted their challenge to rub the potion into my skin. In no time my heart and breathing rate went close to nothing but I was conscious.

Suffice to say it was an experience I would not like to ever repeat.

The second time I visited the Maison I was stripped naked in the sweaty waiting chamber and splashed with holy water. Then I was taken to the mamzelle in her boudoir. She told me to kneel in front of her. When she had finished with me, she told her life story and gave me a 'reading' with the cards and her beautiful fingers.

The Queen of Voodoo

The man kneeling in front of me possessed an evil spirit, f'troo. As plain as the mark on his face. He would get his reward soon enough, though. I could read it when I clasped his head in my hands.

They call me the Voodoo Queen of New Orlins. But I'm really just a businesswoman making profits from my gris-gris pouches, love or hex potions and fortune telling. Like most successful people, I believe it's not just what you do but the style that you do it. I learnt those truths from my predecessors to the throne, Sanité Dédé and Marie Saloppé, as well as my mentor, the King of Voodoo, Dr John Montenee. I was his willing servitor for many years, and he still appears in my dreams demanding to be served until I am wet with my juices. It is only then I wake up knowing that Erzulie, the great mother spirit, possesses me once again.

A sense of theatre, crazy spectacle and outrageous sexual acts are all important, too, in order to make money from Black Magic.

The price of tickets to my annual St John's Day celebration in June, along the shores of Lake Pontchartrain at St John's Bayou, has increased ten-fold over the last few years. Black, white, mulatto, rich, poor, young or old all come now to pay homage to me, the Queen of Queens of Lakeside.

It appeals to them all because I mix holy Catholic prayers and rituals with the old voodoo traditions from Haiti. The rhythmic drumming, repetitive singing and raucous dance my servitors start off cause the crowd to join in the ceremonies, which all forms part of the entertainment. The gods ride them like men ride horses, and in return they are visited by their dead parents and grandparents as they writhe on the floor.

The theatre is provided by me talking in tongues until the crowd are taken over by the spirits. Then I drape my twenty-foot-long snake I call ZoZo around my neck and use her to capture acolytes from the audience, both male and female. Then I bring on a cauldron of boiling water and in front of the crowd I throw in salt, dirt, tarantulas, human bones, a black cat and a black rooster. Finally, I slice a snake into three pieces to represent the Trinity as the final ingredient. Then the prisoners are made to drink my broth. Those less inhibited, because of the alcohol and drugs available, will often strip down and swim in the lake and then noisily couple on the shoreline. Praise be, *Bon Dieu*.

Another large source of income is from this bordello, the Maison Blanche, where currently the ugly English supplicant has his head under the hem of my robe and sucks my toes. The New Orlins elite are regulars here, because even the wealthiest and most powerful citizens have animal needs. They pay not just in money but with information and influence. It's the reason why we are never raided in da Quarters.

I get less money but more gossip from my house visits to the richest ladies. Not a great deal from the wives of the powerful men, of course, but much from their servants and slaves who, in return for my spiritual protection, give me news about their masters' and mistresses' financial, political and sexual affairs.

I am often asked how I can be both a practising Roman Catholic and a devil worshiper. To me, there is little difference between them. I have faith in both... and my god is no devil in disguise.

And I do my nursing work at the Charity Hospital whenever a yellow fever outbreak occurs in New Orlins. Such service to the community makes me feel better every time it happens. May the good god Bondye go with you all.

My supplicant gave a snivel and asked if he could be released. I said he was never a prisoner and when he asked for his reading, I told him, "You will turn into a blackbird flying free in the sky but will end up being carved at the kitchen table."

He snorted and left, shuffling off to his inevitable fate.

Cher Charley

I knew Nell back in Little Brington was not really for me. I enjoyed being with her and some of the silly talks we had. But marriage? If that were to happen, I would only be doing it to make me seem respectable in a place that still looked on me as an outsider. Even though I had lived there for seven years now.

Alice O'Reagan was different. She was well-read, made me feel good about myself and from the beginning of our time on board the *Home* together, my eyes couldn't keep away from her. She always looked back at me over her shoulder whenever we parted and, to my surprise, she never paid such a compliment with handsome Oliver or entertaining Jack. No, it was just me. Cher Charley, as she called me on the last day of the voyage.

It had taken over two years for the three of us to make plans and get our lives in order. Me with the Viscount, Oliver with the Brownlow Estate, which he was now in charge of, and also Jack with Mr Tanqueray. Money to finance our trip, which we thought might go on for a year, was not an obstacle. Oliver had vast wealth now and was doing very little, it seemed, other than some writing for the *New Monthly Magazine* and the *Humorist*. I had my substantial LifeLong share dividends, which I now understood came from Mr Tanqueray. And Jack had worked his artful charms on his employer by saying the journey would bring justice and biblical retribution down on Monks. So, we waved a farewell to England on 10th July 1846.

We were full of anticipation and excitement at catching Monks and dealing with him in whatever way presented itself. Although, we realised our lives would never be the same again after this adventure.

Our little gang certainly learnt a few hard home truths about England on board the *Home* with the O'Reagans, who came from Dublin.

But we learnt the most from Tomás Tighe, who had been forced to give up his small piece of farmland and thatch house in a place called Castlerea to become a tenant of a Protestant absentee landlord a few years back. While he was telling us his story, several other Irish passengers nodded in agreement. It was basically no different for most Catholics around the country.

Tomás said, "Hunger has always been part of rural life in Ireland. We were always poor and treated like peasants by the English. Although, I would say slaves. We lived on potatoes, buttermilk, water, fish and whiskey. But it wasn't until last year that it occurred to me how much my family relied on the potato crop to live. All I knew was I needed one acre of potatoes to feed the four of us for a year. Sometimes the crop failed, but not often, and those times were usually short-lived.

"So, normally we could survive from our food stores built up over previous years and by selling animals or withholding rent.

"Everything changed last October. It had been raining continually for weeks, even more than usual for us. Almost overnight, a dense blue fog settled over the sodden fields. The air smelt like death and next day we saw death itself as the leaves on all the potato plants had turned black and curled. Then they rotted. Our crop was ruined, destroyed by what some locals said was an act of God. The landowners thought the same, except blaming the Catholic faith for bringing a plague down on ourselves.

"The evictions began straight away because many tenants were unable to pay rent. It wasn't just about that, though. The landlords had wanted us fecked out for some time because they realised more profit was to be had hosting sheep rather than people.

"Fortunately, we did have some money savings and so I decided to get out of Ireland straight away with Sally and my boys, Tom and Finn. By the time we left a month ago, the crops had failed again and many of our friends' homes had been destroyed to prevent their reoccupation. All those people would have nowhere else to go other than the workhouse. Although some would at least find shelter in scalpeens, as we call them – that means holes covered in branches, turf-sods, and whatever else was around.

"The cruelty of it all is there's no sympathy or help from the feckin' English whatsoever. Any eggs, butter or beef we had was sent to England while we all starved. And now my family is in exile. Just like all these people here."

The sad mood changed in a minute because a fiddle and a tin whistle came out and the singing and dancing and hard drinking began. Another life lesson for me: you can't keep the Irish down.

Later in the night, I asked Tomás what he would expect to work at in Louisiana.

He said, "I'm going to buy some land, maybe as far upriver as St Louis. No landlord or agent or tax-gatherer to trouble me. No bondage and less misery. It'll all be grand. I'll grow every crop I want, without needing to manure the land ever. I'll never need to feed my pigs again, just let them into the woods to feed themselves, until we need to turn them into bacon. The most important thing is, my family will be free."

All I could think was how ashamed I was to be a fucking Englishman. How could landowners in Ireland treat tenants like slaves? Maybe the Black slave trade had come to an end in the United Kingdom of Great Britain and Ireland, but the Green one certainly had not. It made me think whether or not I should ever again return to England, even with its great buildings. Showing off is not pride or decency.

V

Truth

Gangs of New Orleans: Part 1

I called Ollie, Charley and me a gang. How wrong could I be when I think about Gallatin Street in New Orleans. Most of the gang members round there made Bill Sikes look like a country parson.

"That whole block is where fraud and treachery touches blood," Michael O'Reagan had told us at his poetic best, the first night we had arrived.

The seven of us were having another fine dinner tonight at Antoine's, where we had been staying since we arrived two weeks ago. A time in which the three of us had more fun than we'd had in our entire lives, and we hadn't even moved out of the French Quarter, or *Vieux Carre*, as Antoine's wife, Julie, insisted on calling the area. But most importantly, we had found out some useful information about our old enemy in the bars we drank in at night.

We were told the local bunch that Monks would be most likely be known to was the Live Oak Gang, who were vicious murderers on their good days. Then there was Dutch Pete's Mob, who were even worse. Worser than worse were the Gallatin Street Rangers, run by an Irishman called Archie Murphy. It was a start.

Michael's a gentleman of the first order. A doctor at the local hospital, supporter of the Catholic Church and stand-in father for Terence, James and Alice. All three of them were sound, too. James drank a lot, as I found out to my cost on-board the *Home*. Terence liked his whiskey, but I'd never seen him drunk. Alice was Alice. Only had eyes for Charley from the moment they met. She was a feisty one alright, but caring. Just what Charley needed.

We told them the reason why we had gone west to New Orleans after a week or so eating together on board. In return, they told us stories about a famine in Ireland which was killing people daily from starvation. And it was getting worse. They blamed the English and Queen Victoria for the problems. At first, the three of us shook our heads in disbelief. But too many stories they told rang true. We were ashamed, but it was no different really to how we had been treated by the rich nobs when we were under Fagin's spell.

Michael lived in a grand old house in Magazine Street.

"Close to the Charity and St Patrick's," he told us.

Then he warned us again about Gallatin Street. "It's true, if there's anywhere to start your search for Mr Monks, it's there. But listen to this, all of you. As an old friend once told me, if you have money in your pocket at one end of the street and come out at the other end with your pockets still full and a skull that's still in one piece, then it will be a miracle."

"Well, we're going to have to go there ourselves to find out more. It's been over five years since Monks landed here," I said.

Then Alice spoke up. "Do you really think any of these people you have the names of will even speak to three young Englishmen? They'd kill you on the spot."

She was right, of course, and I said, "Well, I do realise we don't have calling cards or a letter of introduction to the House of Rest for Weary Boatmen, Mother Bunk's Den, and the Sure Enuf Hotel. But I'm confident."

Everybody laughed.

Michael said, "I might have a way to find out more about one of your names, at least."

Interval

In the 1840s, the centre for New Orleans nightlife and sex trade was Gallatin Street, stretching from Ursuline to Barracks. The area was near the docks and located near the present-day French Market.

Herbert Asbury, writing in his 1936 book, *The French Quarter: An Informal History of The New Orleans Underworld*, simply states: 'There was crime and depravity in every inch of Gallatin Street'.

Gallatin Street plus Sanctity Row formed the highest concentration of illegal sex, drinking (licensed or otherwise), violence, robberies, pickpockets and scams in New Orleans. Its location at the edge of the Creole Market, which was city's largest municipal emporium, was the reason for its 'success'. The area buzzed with stalls, streetcars, omnibuses, errand-runners, day-hires, cheap food and amusements. It was open round the clock and cash was its lifeblood. Activities like those attracted transients, curiosity-seekers and adventurers needing bars, cabarets, brothels and gambling dens to satisfy their cravings. Basically, it was a magnet for troublemakers, especially those coming from the nearby shipping wharves at the foot of Esplanade.

There were two types of establishments to be found there. The first was the barrel house, usually a long narrow room lined with casks and filled with liquor of the cheapest quality. Distillers would add 'ingredients' like sulfuric acid and chewing tobacco to add colour or a smoky flavour. Sometimes it was laced with knockout drops, and thieves were hired to rob customers. London Dry Gin it certainly was not.

The second type was dance houses, their main attraction being women for sale. The top floors of these buildings were rented by the night or week by the sex workers, who had to rely solely on the rewards from their skills… and also from robbery.

The average lifespan of a sex worker on Gallatin Street was four years in the 1840s.

Gangs of New Orleans: Part 2

"There's an Archie Murphy who attends Mass every Sunday at St Patrick's with his family," said Michael. "He's a large, imposing man, that's for sure, but always polite. He also gives a large annual donation to the parade along Canal Street every 17th of March.

"There are stories I've heard for sure about where he gets his money from, but it's difficult to believe he's a brothel owner and potentially a murderer. But you never know, do you?"

"Maybe we can go to church then this Sunday, with you all," I said.

I'd spent the last eight years of my life living next door to a church and seeing Bibles and hymn books every day. Even after all that, though, I wouldn't call myself a believer. But I was grateful to the Reverend Edward, Vicar of Ridgmont, for the second chance he gave me in his shelter. I even know the Lord's Prayer and lots of scripture now.

"St Patrick's is a fairly new building, constructed to satisfy the needs of our growing Irish Catholic community here," Michael lectured me. "It's built in the European Gothic style, with a clock tower 185 foot high. Tell Father James those facts, and also that you think it's as impressive as any church you've seen in England, Jack. And remember to praise the murals behind the main altar, especially the one where St Patrick himself is baptising the princess daughters of Ireland's King Laoghaire. Then he'll be wholly impressed and will probably do anything for you, even maybe introducing you to Archie Murphy."

The plan worked like a charm, and the very next Sunday I found myself next to him at the bottom of the front steps as the congregation left. Father James shook our hands in turn and then he introduced me to the gang boss.

I judged that the direct approach was the best policy with a man like this, and so I said straight out to the gang leader, "Sorry to interrupt your Sunday, sir, but Dr O'Reagan from the Charity Hospital told me you might be able to help me find my brother. All our family had lost contact with him many years ago, and I crossed the Atlantic a month or so ago to tell him some sad news about our mother."

"O'Reagan, you say? He's the doctor who saw my daughter through a bad attack of yellow fever a year or so back."

"Yes, Michael's saved lots of lives since he came over from Dublin. So, here goes. Have you met an Englishman called Leeford, or Monks as he sometimes calls himself?

He looks quite distinctive, with a red stain on his skin on the neck and chin. He's very tall, takes himself very seriously and has an eye for a good investment, especially if it's on the dishonest side." I finished with a wink.

"Are you calling me a crook here at the steps of my own church? You forgot to say your brother was crazy and a cheat, as well as being a liar, thief and conman."

In that moment his disposition had changed from family man into a violent thunderstorm. And then he walked off.

Charley and Oliver were not best pleased when I told them what had been said.

"Jack, it was likely to happen because of your big mouth and always ignoring what the other person says. It's what sent the man off in a temper," said Oliver. "We would have done better if the three of us had talked with him in a more friendly way. And remember, Monks is my half-brother, not yours. I have much more need for revenge than you do. So does Charley."

He was right, of course, I hadn't given them a chance. Just thought of myself. The hero.

We split up and I went back to Antoine's. He told me to go for a walk up to Congo Square about five minutes away, where there used to be huge celebrations every Sunday after Mass with loud music, wild dancing and voodoo. But black slaves and free people of colour had now been 'dissuaded' from congregating there for fear of rioting. Some still went, though, selling charms and incense, and telling fortunes. Even street musicians would go there playing jazz, especially at Mardi Gras.

So, I went but soon wished I hadn't because, stupidly, I paid a young mulatto woman to give me a prediction about my future. That was at best a mixed bag, but what upset me was that she appeared to know a lot about my past. And I never talk about it, unlike Oliver and Charley. She churned up thoughts in me about my poor old auntie, Maisie, who raised me because my mother and father didn't want me for reasons I still do not know. She would never speak of it. Was I worthless? Illegitimate? Why wasn't I just flushed away if I was only a burden?

My saviour from my dark mood, fittingly, was a priest.

Father James took Michael aside at the next Sunday Mass and asked him if the stories he had told him about his visitors were true. Michael told me he said he thought there was probably even more than we had confessed, especially about the child prostitution ring that Charley's father had put a stop to. He also said, on my behalf, that I was very sorry if Mr Murphy had taken offence at what I had said at the church.

"But it's Jack's way. Direct, straightforward, no malice. Sort of refreshing in New Orleans, don't you think, Father?"

A month passed, and then Father James got Michael to tell the three of us to attend the next Sunday Mass. If we did go, then afterwards Archie Murphy would pass on some information about Edward Leeford, or the Duke of Southwark, as he now styled himself.

"Cat got your tongue this time, Mr Dawkins?" said Archie, as we sat on a bench opposite St Patrick's. "Let's keep it that way, shall we?"

I nodded.

"I met Leeford on the boat coming from Liverpool. He was intense, even angry, but seemed to know what he was talking about regarding evening entertainments. He had a good idea about moving away from dance halls as front of house brothels for the sailors and drunks. When we met up again a few months later, he said he thought I should get into high-class establishments to catch judges, police and politicians, and their like. People with power and money often like to tread on the side of danger. 'As long as it was safe', he said. 'We should call them bordellos like they did in Europe', he told me. And he was prepared to invest a great deal of money. I let him know we ought to be careful as this type of business is exactly what the Queen Black Witch runs. And we didn't want to be cursed with one of her spells or hexes to turn us both into chickens. Life is tough enough.

"In any case, we bought a number of high-quality houses close to the Charity in the Canal and Basin Street area. He was the perfect silent partner, mainly gambling his life away on the Mississippi Steamboats.

"Everything was fine until a year or so ago. He changed after becoming close friends with a man old enough to be his father, Jeb Cole. And now comes the part of the story explaining why I'm even talking to you. I found out your brother," he said, pointedly looking at Oliver, "had been working with one of my rivals on Barracks Street. He and the madam, Elizabeth Myers, had set up a child prostitution ring that had 'somehow' escaped police attention.

"The reason was plain to see. Leeford was blackmailing several of our important bordello customers to get their silence. When I heard, I sent my rangers around to beat Lizzy senseless and destroy every piece of furnishing and rented room in her main house, as well as setting fire to her precious oyster saloons.

"I would have punished Leeford even more painfully if I could have. But he slipped my net by going upstream on a steamboat to meet his friend. The last I heard of him, from my network, they were doing conman tricks along the Missouri and then north of St Louis on the Mississippi, heading up towards a town called Hannibal.

"I have patience. I can wait until he comes back to deal with him… unless you three want to oblige?"

The King and the Duke

Jeb Cole is the father I never had.

Nobody should say they were tired of the city of New Orleans, but after four years here, I was getting unusually sentimental for my old life in London. Odd for somebody who could be (and has been) described as the coldest of cold fish with few friends to prove it. And it's true, I am not comfortable in society. I don't like people. But that's not to mean I have nothing but revenge and hatred running in my blood.

I realise that to be content I need reaffirmation about my standing, which my mother used to give me constantly. Jeb has made me more secure again.

Much of the last three years has been taken up by the new bordello business I set up with Archie Murphy. I was surprised to hear he had never considered going up market with his numerous employees. But he had not. The opportunities for blackmailing the great and good were immense. And there would be much less fear, violence and death involved with our new custom-built houses. That suited me fine.

But I am alone and lonely and now thirty years old. The only friends I have in the USA are those I meet from time to time in the gambling rooms on the steamboats going up to St Louis and beyond. The invention of that type of transport had transformed the river front communities of New Orleans and brought in many new settlers and immigrants. *More customers for Archie and myself*, I thought.

These days, when I think of the tiny wherries going up and down the Thames, I laugh. That's because transport along the Mississippi is by these large vessels with steam-driven paddle wheels. They tell me the first commercial steamboats started up about forty years ago and transformed New Orleans. The new boats changed the way goods such as cotton, timber, and livestock, which had been carried by unsafe road journeys, all moved to more safe continual movement up and down the river. Yes, the boats could be dangerous because too much steam pressure might build up in the boilers, and then explode. Many others sank each year by colliding with underwater fallen trees, bushes or rocks.

There again, life is a risk. But with the right companions it can be so entertaining.

To pass the time moving along at five miles per hour on a typical eleven-day journey up-river, passengers like me and merchants gamble, drink and are entertained by the so-called fancy women in dancing shows.

I met Jeb in the Southern Belle Saloon on-board the Mississippi Steamboat going between New Orleans and St Louis in 1842. It proved to be the first of many such journeys with the man I realised soon came to know me better than I had ever known myself.

He was about twice my age, bald with grey whiskers and a carpet bag under his chair. We had struck up a conversation over a bottle of Kentucky bourbon when he told me, "I do some doctoring by the layin' on of the hands to cure cancer and paralysis. But my main line is preachin' and missionaryin' around."

He could certainly talk and preach alright.

In turn, I told him about my business interests back in England and now in New Orleans, with evening entertainments like music hall and theatricals.

After we finished in the saloon, we did some gambling. He was good. *Too good*, I thought. And good at marking the cards by scuffing them with his fingernail. Or doing a false shuffle.

Personally, I've never once tried to manipulate the cards on land. I was too scared of being grabbed like those five card sharps who were caught in the act a few years back and hanged by a lynch mob for their crimes.

But riverboats are ideal for avoiding any legal problems because the waters on the Mississippi River are not regulated. That means gambling con artists – cheats, that is – can play and travel unchecked. Over the years I got to know some well-known card sharps who never left the boats to avoid being arrested.

Jeb was not just a clever cheat, he was successful because he would play the part of an innocent, slightly simple, born loser. He had a way of asking foolish questions and sharing confidences with people he identified as being 'suckers ripe for burning'. They could be preachers or soldiers. He did not care as long as they fell hard for his stage act. Needless to say, their money invariably ended up in his carpetbag.

When not playing poker, his favourite game was three-card-monte, or find the lady. I was often his shill while Jeb picked up one of the cards with one hand, and two with the other. Then we would simply misdirect the mark, so he followed the wrong card from the very beginning. He was only called out once in all our journeys together on the steamboats. And that was by a well-dressed Irishman who quietly said to him, "Don't try to con an O'Connor, sir, or you will need a feckin' wheelchair to disembark."

Jeb has more stories inside his head waiting to burst out than any other person I have ever met. None of them might have been true, but he could make me laugh like nobody else had ever done. He was like Shakespeare's Falstaff to my Prince Hal, and I told him so. The father I wished I had been granted by God.

We would soon be back in New Orleans. Back to the reality of the seedy world of Gallatin Street, Archie Murphy and my secret business partner Lizzie Myers. *It's time for me to move on*, I thought.

When I realised that simple fact, I finally told Jeb the story about me, my father and Oliver. How I had tried to cheat my half-brother out of his unpardonable inheritance. After all, I was the firstborn child. I've always felt everything left to the world by my father should have been for me, not his pathetic baby. That weak excuse for a man was a coward who ran away for some underage girl, who he may or may not have married. All as a result of his behaviour, I've been torn from my life in England and now I am hunted and despised by society. My heart breaks even at the thought of the little bastard, Oliver, taking what is rightfully mine. All my dear mother cherished and wanted for me.

Jeb replied, "Now, you have a great sob story there, son. And you tell it fine. The duke and Old King Cole, with the help of Mr Shakespeare, can definitely use it to fleece some suckers in the small towns alongside the riverbank."

Elizabeth Myers

My parents were both German, but I was born in New Orleans where they emigrated to in 1808. Prussia was poor then because of losing to Napoleon at a place called Jena and having to pay crippling amounts of money to the French. Father felt humiliated by the defeat and by losing his farm, like so many of his friends.

My land-owning family was now working class and, unlike the richer middle classes of Prussia, they could not follow the despicable Hanoverians to England. Instead, they travelled steerage to Louisiana in the same way as about seven thousand others.

Like many other Germans we settled in the Third District, known to us as Little Saxony. Father got a job in a slaughterhouse and, like most other German families, my brother Peter was sent to fetch a bucket of city beer at the end of every day, which we all drank with dinner. He was two years older than me and much more German. I, on the other hand, liked doing things not just involving drinking cheap alcohol, singing in friendship groups, going to church and playing endless games of cards on a Sunday.

For this exact reason, I did not get on well with either my mother or father. I felt I was an American. So as soon as I could, I left home.

I started as a gentlelady of the night, as we were called. I presented no threat, as did some white Irish prostitutes in the streets like 'Bricktop' Jackson or Bridget Fury, who were not to be crossed if you wanted to keep your body in one piece at the end of service.

Thank God, I never had to sink so low as those black whores did on Smokey Row. They charged as little as twenty cents per John for some 'love' in an indoor den. But many chose to sit outside in the street sitting on wooden crates and spitting out wads of tobacco while waiting for potential customers to pass by.

"Ten cents," they'd shout. Yes, just ten cents a push from men who didn't mind a bit of public exhibition and would do the deed right on the street. I was never so desperate. No woman should ever be so desperate.

With time my gentle approach, which just meant letting the men talk and moan about their lives, began to pay off. Within three months I had a long list of regulars, a crib of my own and food on the table.

So, I became an accomplished prostitute from the very beginning. I was also shrewd with the rewards I got for my labours. But I'm first to admit, unless I'm with a trusted customer, that I have a short temper and can be violent with those who cross me. As those customers trying to short-change me found out when meeting my knife, which

I call Fritz, with its double-ended five-inch blade. Being brutal like that was a normal part of life in Gallatin Street. A lesson in life I learnt when I became intimately involved with the Irishman, as I called him. Our relationship was mutually beneficial. He gave me protection and I gave him whatever he wanted.

All was good until Mr Murphy killed my brother, Peter. They had had a drunken shouting match in Customhouse Street. Archie pulled a gun and shot Peter in the face. He died ten days later. Even though there were eyewitnesses to tell what had happened, Archie walked free, claiming self-defence.

I cut all business and romantic dealings with the Irishman and decided it was time to become respectable in order to find a good husband. I found him soon enough. His name was Tom Brady, and he was a clerk in the City Treasurer's office.

He took me wherever and whenever I wanted during our whirlwind six months together. We stayed most weekends at out-of-state luxurious hotels. It was a side of life I had no idea about given my background. So, I resolved to emulate *der Komfort* I was experiencing in some new-style brothels I would commission and call Chateaux. I began to hire foreign girls in order to increase the appeal to upscale customers. They have particular tastes for sampling the exotic, I have found. I also decided to open some oyster bars in the basements of a few saloons I called Lizzies, as a small vanity I felt I deserved.

All was good until this unusual English creature called Leeford became a business partner with Mr Murphy, and they decided to open some high-class brothels of their own.

I wanted to make sure we did not take each other's business. So, just like I had met with the powerful Marie Laveau, Voodoo Queen and bordello owner, I met with Leeford. But unlike the mamzelle, I found him to be very insecure. *He's one who badly needs the attentions of one of my French ladies, or even one of my strong German boys*, I thought. It was too difficult to read which he would prefer.

I started by sending both Adelle and Paul to talk to him. He kept both for what became a regular arrangement. He was apparently a hard taskmaster but rarely talked. Until one day he asked them if I dealt with anyone younger, say, twelve years old.

I decided to confront him and told him child prostitution was a step too far for me.

He simply laughed and said, "I ran a ring like that in London. Very lucrative, it was. You should think twice before you take the moral high ground. We are lost souls anyway." He then offered to invest and pass on small but important details about how to maximise profits and avoid prosecution.

Our business together lasted a year or so until Mr Murphy learnt of his partner's activities with me. Of which he knew nothing.

I was beaten with cudgels by his men, my Chateaux were destroyed, and the Lizzies were burned down.

Leeford had slipped away like the snake he was into the night, probably on a riverboat. And I never heard from him again.

As soon as I recovered my health, I left for New York. Good business to be had there, I was sure.

JIM THOMAS

I arrived at Pontchartrain railway station just outside New Orleans city about nine months ago to start a new life as a free black man. I got out of that place as quickly as possible, though, because of the devil-worshipping voodoo orgies which are said to be held on the shores of the lake. Stories of depravities there had even reached my plantation slave friends a hundred and fifty miles away.

My mother was born in the Kingdom of Dahomey on the slave coast of West Africa, and transported to Mobile, Alabama at the age of sixteen in 1812. She died there one year ago, on the day before I was made a freeman by my master.

Buying negroes in exchange for weapons, opium, gold and gunpowder had been commonplace for Europeans since the sixteenth century. The human cargo often ended up in the Americas as slaves because Blacks were, and still are, good cheap labour for doing back-breaking jobs on plantations and also for the casual gratification of their masters and families. My mother was one of those unfortunate ones.

For whatever reason, maybe due to some local revolts in the Caribbean plantations, white society began to develop a conscience about slavery in the first ten years of the new century, and 'An Act Prohibiting Importation of Slaves' in the United States came into force in 1808.

In reality, the practice has still not been stamped out even now, in 1846.

My mother was bought in a slave market in Africa and then transported on a schooner specially built and equipped to minimise losses of its human cargo on its long journey west. She later told me that the *Clovis* was commissioned by an Irish-American called Patrick Meaher, who owned a shipyard in Mobile. Its first destination abroad was the slave market in Ouidah and then, loaded with human cargo, she set sail from there in March arriving back home in the United States during May.

The captain carried $13,000 in gold to purchase Africans and bought 100 men for $100 each and 50 women for $2500. All of them were Tarkbars captured in an Ashanti raid during the local tribal wars.

After the *Clovis* returned to the United States, the slaves were distributed quietly to the financial backers of the venture. Patrick Meaher kept thirty captives to work on his property north of Mobile. My mother was one of those made to serve the master at his table and in his family beds.

I was called a child of the plantation. In other words, the offspring of my black enslaved mother and the brother of Michael Meaher, her owner. She never told me if I was born out of rape. What could I have done even if I knew?

So, my lot was to be a mulatto, albeit one with an ebony black skin unlike so many others. Not that I wanted to be, but even with a lighter skin I could never have been part of whitey society.

Compared to many who were slaves in Louisiana, most of us were treated well if we were polite, obedient and did not try to escape. Some, though, often begged for mercy from their overseer in the cotton fields.

Resistance to our captivity took many forms on the plantation. Some slaves performed careless work or destroyed property or faked illness. Some even became fugitive runaways in order to rejoin family members living nearby. Others ran because they wanted to avoid the harsh working conditions in the fields during the growing season and the punishment beatings or collarings that could happen at the overseer's whim. But it was whippings mainly, or a single crippled foot, or the sickening nose slit. Worst of all was doing time on the treadmill. This was a torture device, which was supposed to improve the work ethic and was basically a huge turning wheel built with thick, splintering wooden slats. If you were accused of laziness (or what slave owners called the 'negro disease'), you'd end up hung by the hands from a plank and forced to 'dance' the treadmill barefoot, often for hours. If a slave fell or lost their step, they would be battered on their chest, feet and shins by the wooden planks until they were senseless, before being cut down so they could work next day.

And any woman slave could be held down and knocked up by a 'boss' anytime the feeling took them. It took them often.

I saw and heard about these barbarities handed out by Whites myself while growing up on the Mobile plantation. I also realised that some favour was being shown to me, almost certainly because of being a son of the master's family. So, I was not put out into the cotton fields to work, instead I became a domestic servant. The days were long, the tasks easy and I was actually treated with more respect by the family and the slaves than the 'poor white trash' – these were the non-black servants, many of them Irish, who were deemed the dregs of society because they had not taken proper advantage of being white. *Strange world*, I was beginning to think. Especially as the real 'white trash' were the rich ones, in my view.

After about the age of twelve I was given some reading and writing. In part this was done so I could read the Bible and become a true Christian. But it was also to train me to perform tasks such as record-keeping. The best education I got, though, was from my mother and her friend, Joseph, who had got hold of a banjo. He taught me how to play the tribal rhythms commonplace in Africa, all in the fast, crazy, energetic way he called 'jass'. It lifted me and also everyone I knew that heard it. Actually, it helped me to become more accepted on the plantation by the other slaves who, up until then, had called me 'Massa's Houseboi'. But at least not 'white trash', I suppose.

Even Samuel, the bare-knuckle champion of our plantation, became my friend. A six-foot tall man from Mandinka, who was so powerful that he had won two 'Battles Royales' and earnt Master a great deal of money.

So, his day-to-day duties were very light. His night duties were a bit more strenuous.

"A pleasure to be of service to the whole family," he told me, smiling, one day.

My mother never married, although many asked her. I don't know why, and it's the same for me. Thirty years old without a wife? Maybe things will change once I start playing my banjo in the clubs and saloons. It is, after all, the reason I came here to New Orleans, the home of jass. No place else was like it for a musician.

In the last three months I have earnt a lot of money from my performances in every type of musical outlet there is here. And so I decided to treat myself to a performance at the Théâtre d'Orléans down between Royal and Bourbon. Tonight, the world famous soprano *mademoiselle* Julie Calvé was playing the part of Pauline in Donizetti's *Les martyrs*. I settled down, finding myself seated next to a lively Englishman called Jack, who told me immediately that he'd been dragged here by the three friends next to him. His personality was infectious and at the interval the five of us took a drink together.

It turned out we were all going on the Mississippi Steamboat next week to St Louis. Me for providing musical entertainment in the Southern Belle saloon, them for seeking out an old acquaintance. I didn't realise at the time what an adventure that was going to turn out to be for Jim Thomas Washington.

VI

Revenge

The Three Musketeers

Oliver, Jack and Charley had come to see the O'Reagans before they left in two days' time on their journey up the Mississippi. They were drinking whiskey with Michael in the sitting room when Alice came in waving a book and shrieking with delight.

"The English translation of the best adventure story ever written has finally arrived. *Les Trois Mousquetaires*, by Alexandre Dumas."

To which Jack replied, "Let's hope it's better than the four-act opera you made us go to last week. All in French, set in Armenia – wherever that is – and you don't even get to see the lions tear the Christians apart at the end. Longest three hours of my life."

Michael and Oliver burst out laughing. Charley tried to suppress because Alice was glaring at him.

Then she said, "You're a philistine, Jack Dawkins. The entertainment on the steamboat will no doubt suit you better. High kicks and low cards."

"And we'll be getting some good music from Jim, too, don't forget," said Oliver.

But Alice wasn't finished yet. "The ironic thing is that the three of you are just like the three main characters in this book." She waved it around again. "Jack, you're Porthos, the extrovert who loves good times, food and anyone who will listen to his endless chatter. You're Athos, Oliver, noble and handsome but melancholic, trying to bury the memories of his past in drink. My cher, Charley, you are Aramis. In two minds about everything. Grazier or adventurer. Wherryman or pickpocket. But most of all, a good friend."

"And what about the villain in the book, Alice? There has to be an evil villain in a swashbuckler like I bet this is," Michael said.

"Of course, there is," replied Alice. "He's called Cardinal Richelieu, an adviser to the king, who is described as diabolical and somebody who never hesitates to use any means possible to achieve his evil aims."

The three musketeers said in unison, "Monks."

Planning the campaign to find Monks and getting revenge had not taken long. First, a steamboat to St Louis. Then, a quick look for any traces of him along the first thirty miles of the Missouri River, maybe to St Charles and close by towns. And finally, back to the Mississippi for a trip to Hannibal, which Archie Murphy had told us was the direction our Richelieu was heading towards.

The Mississippi Steamboat was one of the more luxurious vessels around. Like all the others, it had a large paddlewheel in the back with wide decks stacked one on top of another, each becoming narrower as you moved to the top. It was like a tiered wedding cake.

There were a couple of funnels belching out black smoke from the wood burning. And when the wind was right it was normal to get a mouthful of stinking fuel ash.

Passengers boarded the boat on the lower deck, which was open because it's where the cotton bales and barrels of sugar and molasses were stored. We were told it was freight paying the bills. Not us.

There were also some $3 deck passengers who had to bring their own food and took their chances with the elements because they lived outside next to the freight and animals.

Meanwhile, on the upper decks the cabin passengers like us paid double what the deck passengers did. But we had our own private rooms, ate in a stately dining room and drank in the saloon with gambling tables. There was also music every night. That's where we saw Jim again, on our first night on board.

He was good. Very good. And the boozers and gamblers loved him. It was a different world on the boat from living in downtown New Orleans. Here there was no prejudice against Blacks, unless you were a runaway slave, that is.

We had many good evenings with Jim. We even called him the Fourth Musketeer.

He warned us about getting our stuff stolen or taken. We said we could retaliate in kind if that happened because of our childhood training. He also let us know who the professional card sharps were, and when to stand up and leave a table. And to always carry a knife.

The captain would occasionally come into the

Southern Belle for a drink and so we asked him if anybody like Monks – British, tall, red birthmark – had ever been seen on board.

"Sounds like the duke to me," said Captain Sanders. "He and his gambling buddy – Old Man Cole, we called him – used to be regulars on board here until about a year ago. They were both a pair of cheats, we knew, but sometimes to stop big trouble it's best to turn a blind eye to little troubles, I've found. The bald one was always preaching about the Good Lord loving supplicants with clean teeth to whoever was not only gullible enough to listen to his bullcrap, but also then to purchase some of his cream to remove tartar. And, as no doubt the customers found once off the boat, it was a good enamel remover, too.

"The duke was content to play the card tables and drink whiskey for most of the time. Last time I saw them was in St Louis, carrying enough luggage to sink a ship. I guess it was the costumes and stage props they needed for their scenes from Shakespeare, as they called it."

We docked about three days after hearing this news and got ready to go on a short trip by another steamboat on the Missouri River that embarked just to the north side of St Louis.

Jim's plan had been to spend some time performing in the city to earn money and improve his piano playing. But what he wanted to do the most was to start composing his own music in the blues style, in the place where it had begun.

Before doing that, we convinced him to spend a week with us on the boat trying to pick up any trail of Monks.

JIM THOMAS: FUGITIVE

One thing I will tell my children is never to like an Englishman. They can be charming and good company, yes. But never get to like them.

Why am I saying this? Because my diversion up the Missouri River with Jack, Oliver and Charley on the *James Morrison* steamboat turned into a particular hell for me.

To think, I could be playing the blues in St Louis. Instead, I'm in a city jail cell on Main Street, in the heart of St Charles, within spitting distance of a whipping post set up by the last sheriff here twenty years ago. It is still used, I'm told.

The visit had started off so well, too, yesterday. We got two rooms at Chambers Hotel on South Main. Me with Charley and Oliver with Jack. We decided the three of them would go explore how this city was regarding free Blacks with Whites. It was not New Orleans, after all.

Before they left, the boys checked with the front desk, asking the owner if he had ever seen anybody fitting Monks' description in the city over the last year or so.

He said not to his knowledge and that the three of them were the first English to stay. Then they asked where they might find out any information at all about a pair of actors giving theatrical performances of one sort or another. He told them to go to the Old Mill towards the bottom of South Main, near Boonslick. It was the place to go for local information because farmers from all over congregated there to share gossip and then go shopping.

They went to the Mill, but nobody could remember any plays being put on in St Charles by any Englishmen, who were few and far between here anyway. Unlike Germans, who were many and everywhere. All everyone was talking about was a man they called Injun Joe. A nasty, evil character by all accounts.

"Bad blood makes you do evil things," one farmer said.

Another chimed in with, "Booze and the Red Indian never mix well." He then went on, "He deserved to die in the cave he was locked up in. Murderer, grave robber, bully and liar. Starvation was too good an end for him, I'm thinking."

When the three came back to the hotel they were full of the stories about Injun Joe.

Jack said, "What sort of country is this we've come to? No wonder Monks had chosen here to live. He's welcome to it, as far as I'm concerned."

Their good news was that from looking around it seemed like Blacks were well accepted in the city. *Presumably only if you're a free man like me*, I thought.

So, we all went together to visit the rest of St Charles and get some food and drink. But I kept my manumission papers signed by Mr Meaher very close to my chest.

First, we went to the printing shop for the *Western Star* newspaper, close to the blacksmiths, again on South Main. Jack suggested that if Monks and friend were going to put performances on anywhere, they would need some playbills made up to let people know where and when they were on.

The *Western Star* office was small and chaotic, with newly printed pages everywhere. Some on the floor, some on the central desk and some stuck up on the walls. We got there and a small, squint-eyed man with blackened ink fingers greeted us like old friends. Yes, he did remember somebody with a red face birthmark and English accent ordering some handbills.

One was to advertise three performances close to the Court House in St Peter's, about ten miles west from here, starring David Garrick the younger and Edmund Kean the elder, straight from the London theatre. In scenes from Shakespeare and other comedies. Admission fifty cent. No women or children allowed.

"I remember it word for word because I was thinking, *that baloney will last just one night, at most.*"

The second was an invitation to attend a lecture by Professor Franz Gall, inventor of the science of phrenology along with his assistant, Spurzheim. Get to know your mind better. Improve your luck. And live a longer life. All by observing and feeling your skull. Entrance fifty cents with personalised brain charts for only twenty-five cents.

"I was thinking of getting a reading for myself."

The third handbill was notice of a temperance meeting hosted by the world famous Capuchin priest, Father

Theobold Mathew, all the way from Ireland. Limited spaces only. Twenty cents entry with a personal confession at thirty cents.

The last one was a poster advertising the duke and king's supernatural powers for water and gold divination.

While Charley and Oliver were dealing with the obviously German printer, Jack and I were looking at the wall covered in posters to see if any clues were right in front of our eyes. As soon as I saw one of them, I realised I might be in for trouble. Dated March 1846, it said:

Fugitive slave from the St Jaques plantation close to New Orleans is wanted by the Subscriber. On 1st January a negro man named James, or Jim, about thirty years of age, five foot ten inches tall, became a runaway. Anyone bringing him to me alive shall have $5 reward or $15 for his head only. Signed John Armistead.

At the top of the bill was a sketch drawing.

We thanked the printer and left. As always, Jack was the first to say it.

"That drawing looked a lot like you, Jim."

I nodded and said, "Let's hope they've all forgotten. But maybe I should move on from here straight back to St Louis."

They agreed, but first we went to the California House saloon near the top end of South Main for some beer. The plan then was to go to Eckert's Tavern and Inn for some dinner. It didn't work out that way.

Let me put the case for my defence first. For the first twenty-eight years of my life I drank no alcohol whatsoever. In the last year or so I've drunk some beer to be social in the bars and saloons I've played in. But tonight, those likeable English boys served rounds of table shots. That's four Kentuckys and four brews apiece. So when we left the California House, I was louder than I normally am. I began singing 'The Boatman's Dance' at the top of my voice.

Repeatedly.

The English laughed until the printer we had met earlier approached us with a large man, who introduced himself as Sheriff John Gilbert.

"He's the fugitive negro on the poster, Sheriff. Can I claim the reward?"

The lawman turned to me. "Enjoying yourself, Jim? Or is it James? Or just Fugitive? In any case, you'll be enjoying my hospitality at the City Jail for as long as it takes for you to sober up and prove you're not a runaway to the District Judge."

TWIST

What have we done to Jim? I thought.

In my past life in London under Fagin's control, I had only escaped going to prison by the intervention of Mr Brownlow.

But I had been locked away much earlier than that by Sowerberry, the undertaker, after I had been released from the workhouse. And all just because I finally attacked his little bully boy, Claypole. The fight started because he goaded me about my dear mother.

"What did she die of, Work'us? Of a broken heart over some evil rogue who left his wife for a scullery maid? She was a real bad'un."

Something like that, anyway. I can't remember because I lost control, beating him with my fists until Sowerberry and wife dragged me struggling and shouting into the dust-cellar, where they imprisoned me and then beat me with a cane. After that they threw me into my workshop sleeping room. But I managed to undo the door fixings with some tools during the night and left for London at first light.

My first real time in jail was seeing Fagin, who had been sentenced to death for his crimes. On his miserable last night alive, Mr Brownlow and I visited his filthy cell to find the papers verifying my true identity as a Leeford, after Monks had passed them on to the bag of bones.

That was the moment my new life started, because Mr Brownlow adopted me as his son. And now I'm here in a hotel room in St Charles while my friend is in jail because I got him drunk.

In the morning, we went straight to the jail to vouch for Jim as a freeman and character of the highest order.

The sheriff greeted us with a knowing smile. "I know why you're here, but it can't happen at the moment. James – or Jim, as he prefers – has showed his signed papers freeing him from slavery, alright. The problem is they might be a forgery. We've seen that many times here. And really the handbill Ebeling the printer had on his wall was pretty conclusive. Name, Jim. Slave in New Orleans. Right age and height. Image of the sketch. I don't believe in coincidences."

"So how can we sort this out?" said Jack straight away. "We know he's no runaway. He's been performing in New Orleans on banjo and piano for the last year or so."

"Music cuts no ice, son," the sheriff replied. "At very least we'll have to get the District Judge to inspect them. But he might want proof from the owner of Jim himself. Before you say it, Judge Millington is on the circuit for the neighbourhood courts. And he's away for another day or so. When he gets back, he'll be in the courthouse close to the old Capitol Building."

Telling Jim this news was difficult. He said all he could do was pray. And that we should do the same.

We did, and at yet another Jack suggestion we decided to go the short journey to St Peter's to try to pick up the trail of Monks.

Late morning, we got on a stagecoach at Eckert's Tavern for a very bumpy two hour ride to what turned out to be no more than a provincial village.

It would not take long to find out anything here. Anyway, we walked quickly to the courtroom because it was the place that was advertised on the playbill.

A man calling himself the circuit clerk remembered it all too well.

"The performers called themselves the king and the duke and rigged up their own stage just over there outside the church ground. Their play was so bad, so laughably bad, that word of mouth did the rest. It went on for three nights, mainly because one of them took all his clothes off on stage. Although women had been warned off, many did come in the end and some of them applauded. Virtually everyone I know, including from the farms around, laid out their half dollars, some more than once, to watch this live steamboat crash.

"Of course, the real losers were the audience. They all had paid hard-earnt cash on an evening that was a complete embarrassment to themselves and to the actors, I would have thought. But who would admit it? And that was the last we saw of the king and duke, thank God."

Fortunately, Judge Millington was back the next day to look over Jim's manumission papers. At the start he was dubious about it all, until we described why we were here in the first place.

"The king and the duke, you say? Liars, cheats and twisted conmen, I hear on my travels." He turned to Jim. "I'm tending to believe your story now. Catching those crooks would do our community a service. I am sorry for your inconvenience, Mr Washington, but you must understand we have to take all fugitive slave cases very seriously. Or our society might fold. I wish you well on your journey."

The next day we boarded the *James Morrison* to get back to St Louis.

It was a relatively short trip, but we were well aware steamboats travelling on the Missouri did not have a long lifespan. Maybe two or three years. Sandbanks, submerged trees and explosions were the main causes. I wondered if our luck might run out.

Ours did not sink, but the *Walter Scott* was not so lucky. We came close by it crippled on a rock and snagged too by a submerged tree. There were men on board. But we did not stop. I can only hope some decent souls came by to help them as we moved on towards our destination. Not home, but a staging post to deal with Monks in Hannibal.

Meanwhile, Jim went back to St Louis to play music.

THE KING AND THE DUKE: THE BROTHERS WILKS

Another of my nine lives came to an end on the night that Archie Murphy took his violent revenge on my occasional partner, Lizzie.

As is normal for me, I was one step ahead of everyone and had bought yet another steamboat ticket headed for St Louis. I had arranged to meet Jeb there in a hotel, where we hoped to put our final plans in place to fleece unwary marks in every small town along the Mississippi and the Missouri.

Jeb had many small money scams in mind, which we would unleash for just a few days here and a few days there.

"Keeping on the move will prevent any misunderstandings with the locals from turning into violence on our precious selves. I learnt that lesson many moons ago. Sometimes people just don't understand that we're trying to do some good by making their sad lives more interesting," he said before we got on the boat to St Charles from St Louis.

He had many ways in mind of gripping his 'congregations', as he called them. His favourite cons were those where he'd preach to the unconverted. Not about God, of course. More about knowing thyself and reaching a place where you could become the best person you could be. He certainly knew what we all really wanted to know – that is, how to get one up on our brothers, sisters and neighbours.

He tried one of his 'performances', as he called them, on the steamboat. That one was to preach what even I thought was a step too far – that is, to 'clean teeth brings you closer to the Good Lord'. And he had just the stuff to 'clean your pegs'. He called it RubOut, a paste you applied to your teeth to remove unsightly tartar. He had brought with him lots of small tin cans containing a grey cream we later realised took off enamel as well as tartar. Fortunately, the complaints came in just as we came into St Charles. We got away with an extra $50 in our pockets. Not much in terms of my own wealth, but it was the fun and excitement that made it worthwhile. The feeling was just like taking a bottle of Zeus.

St Charles was not the place for scams to be successful, we thought. Too well educated because German accents and language were everywhere. We needed a few one-horse towns full of American provincials and farmers.

As soon as we got into the city, we searched for a printing shop so we could get some playbills and handbills. We found the *Western Star* newspaper office on South Main (where all of commercial life lived in St Charles, I soon realised) and a printer, too. His rates were cheap, much to my surprise, and we got fifty copies each of the four scams we wanted to try.

But first we asked about small towns and farming areas that were about ten miles away.

He said, "St Peter's is closest but St Paul's and Old Monroe are possibilities if you want to travel a bit further."

We paid the money, collected the handbills and then went into the blacksmith's about two minutes away to rent out a horse and wagon to take our luggage to wherever life took us.

Life actually took us to a space across the street from the courthouse in St Peter's. We passed our fliers out in the few shops and bars there were there, and hoped for the best at half a dollar a head.

We got just six dollars on opening night. Doing the balcony scene from *Romeo and Juliet*, *Hamlet's* soliloquy, even the sword fight from *Richard III* got us catcalls and rotten vegetables. Then, in frustration, I did *King Lear's* 'blow winds and crack your cheeks' speech while taking all my clothes off and then dancing wildly and farting out very loud. All performed butt naked on the stage. That got their attention alright. Then they laughed and, as we found out the next night, they had told their friends and neighbours about the performance. We earnt $50 our second night and $85 on our third and final night. Who would have thought there would be so many lovers of the words of the Great Bard in Smalltown?

Next, we took ourselves up to St Paul's, where we tried the temperance meeting routine. Jeb as an Irish priest shouting, "God only exists if you believe in him", and me as a shill in the crowd shouting, "Praise Be" or "Thank you, Lord", and at the climax of the holy preach running up to Jeb and then turning towards the audience to swear I'd never drink whiskey again.

"And who will join me in making a donation to Father Mathew's charity for homeless children?"

A surprising number did so on the first two nights. But after the second we rode like the wind out of town back to St Charles because some nosey old lady caught us swigging bottles of Bourbon outside our wagon, where we'd been sleeping.

From St Charles we went back to St Louis and then up the Mississippi towards a place called Hannibal, about two days away on a steamboat.

We stopped off at a few small towns on the way to see if there were any brains around. We were not disappointed, and so it actually took us a few months to reach our real destination.

Glascock's Landing on the western shore of the Mississippi is where we finally disembarked after a river journey, which for the last five miles passed lumber yards after sawmills after more lumber yards. And then we headed towards Main Street, where there was a hotel and a bar the steamboat captain had told us about. This place was even a town? *Probably more horses and livestock than its two thousand inhabitants*, I thought to myself. It was still what Jeb called a one-horse town, though.

We booked two rooms and then went along the street to a bar called O'Malleys on the north end of Main.

Jeb went up to get some Kentuckys. The barkeep was serving and talking to another couple of customers.

"Anyway, the funeral's in two days. The family has waited a while for his two brothers to arrive from England, but no sign of them yet."

Jeb knows when to listen and learn. He has an instinct.

"Well, Paddy," said one of the customers. "Peter Wilks is a real loss to us all and the girls. He never even got to see his brother, William, who it's said is deaf and dumb. Hadn't seen the older brother, Harvey, since they were children. That family have had some bad luck this past year. Peter's brother, George, and his wife both died, as you know. It's those three nieces who will be most upset."

Paddy replied, "You're not wrong, Sean. I reckon Mary Jane will be the one crying most but the two younger ones will be very hurt, too. They all loved their Uncle Peter. At least the girls will come into a very decent inheritance, but the brothers get the property, I hear."

Such information was more than enough to get Jeb's wheels turning. He sat down, put the four Kentuckys he had bought in front of us and smiled. We drank them slowly and savoured the continuing conversation at the bar.

The Brothers Wilks were about to be born.

Dr Robinson

The three Wilks girls had been through a very bad year. First, there was their father dying because of a mosquito bite. Then their mother passing on a few weeks later. There is no such ailment as a broken heart, but it might well have been what happened to Lily Wilks.

Her last wish was that her three daughters were to be left in the capable hands of Peter, who was George's brother.

Peter was a good person, God rest him, but someone who did not like spending his money overmuch, especially on legal fees.

"Hannibal's nothing more than a town full of lawyers and sawyers these days," he would say. And there's no doubt his cash was hard-earnt from turning animal skins into leather. It was a dirty and dangerous occupation, for sure, because the chemicals used to disinfect the hides and to strip the animal skins away smelled like they were top-class killers. It seemed like his workshop was always full of bad eggs and burning coal. And he worked in that putrid air for thirty years until a month or two ago when his lungs began to fail and eventually could no longer function.

Until he was buried, his money and property belonged to nobody. But we all knew in Hannibal that the girls would get substantial inheritances. Maybe even the property and land, unless the two brothers from England turned up.

The funeral had been delayed so Peter's living brothers could get here. A message had been sent to England but there was no sign of them yet and the funeral had been arranged for three days' time. I was looking forward to meeting William and Harvey because my mother came from England. So, I love a British accent when I hear one.

I say that because twenty-four hours later, just before I was leaving to go up country to deliver some babies, two conmen came into the Wilks girls' lives.

The one who called himself Harvey could have been an old tramp. And he really had the worst English accent I have ever heard. The other, younger one, made a mockery of the deaf and dumb. Grunting and rolling eyes with the occasional drool.

They had been with the girls for the morning when I arrived just before leaving town. Mary Jane had taken a particular liking to them because they told them stories about Peter when he was young. *All sweet manure*, I thought. But I would also admit they knew a lot about everything to do with the Wilks. Especially the money. I took the girls aside and told them to beware and that they were crooks. But they would have none of it. I left telling them I would be back from my duties with the expectant mothers as soon as possible.

When I got back the next evening, I was horrified to hear how quickly those two hucksters had got a grasp of $6000 the girls had given them in a cloth bag. My friend, Levi Bell, who was Peter's lawyer, gave me even worse news.

"Those two devils put up bills of sale on the properties yesterday, with Mary Jane's permission. She's grieving hard and's just plain irrational at the moment. The auction of the house, land and furniture is taking place the day after the burial. What the crooks don't understand is that nobody don't have to pay for the things they buy until a whole day after the auction on account of the short notice. And we can fix it so it's longer. Those two won't leave without all of that cash burning a hole in their pockets. So, we have to be quick and pray for a miracle like both of them dropping dead. Or hope the real brothers turn up."

I was so mad I went straight to the girls and said that I wash my hands of the matter. And I warned them, "A time's coming when you're going to feel sick whenever you think of this day, unless you change your minds about these two conmen."

The funeral service was to be held at noon in the Melpontian Hall on the corner of Centre and Third. Funny how a place used for slave auctions can double as a place of worship for the Trinity Church. But it does. The whole town was likely to come. And it did.

As the coffin was brought in, a borrowed melodeon started up and everybody sang 'To Be A Pilgrim' as loud as they could. Then the Reverend Hobson stood up, slowly and solemnly, and began to talk. It was a good sermon and respectful to Peter. He would surely go to heaven with such a send-off.

Without invitation, unless Mary Jane had told him to do it, the brother Harvey began to preach.

"Fellow mourners," he started. "It is with a sad British heart I speak about my brother, Peter. When we lived in England, we were inseparable. And although I haven't seen him for many years, I still love him even now he's gone. As does my brother, William."

The tall man with a red birthmark (or was it an unusual scar?) on his face nodded and grunted, as he got up to stand side by side with his brother at the front of the congregation.

Then, three young men in the crowd stood up and one of them shouted, "That man is no more an Englishman than I am an American living on the moon. And the grunting one is a thief and murderer and employs child prostitutes in his brothels in New Orleans."

Then all hell broke loose.

John Clemens: The Justice of the Peace

I don't think I have much longer to live but it's been a good life, made even better by my wife of twenty-five years, Jane. We had seven children together but only four are with us still. I am proud of them all. I wish I could be there to see what becomes of Orion, Pamela, Samuel, and Henry. Will they marry well? Become famous? Have dozens of children between them? I'll never know. Henry Robinson says it's pneumonia and we both know what that means.

I did my last job as a JP and District Judge just a week ago. Although, the law was taken out of my hands. It always is when a mob realises it has all the power and the one man with a certificate or two is nothing more than a fly on the wall.

Peter Wilks' funeral turned into the type of send-off he would have hated. All because of those petty conmen who Mary Jane bought into lock, stock and barrel. When the loud shout from the congregation came, the old bald one just looked confused but the ugly one stood rigid to the spot. More rooted than the white oak tree in our garden. Mouth opening and closing like a fish on the sand with no sound coming out. Horror on his face making him look like a ghost with a bloody neck and cheek.

The three Englishmen (as I found they were later that day, when they came to our house for dinner) ran as one to the front of the congregation and began beating the living daylights out of him with their fists until they were pulled off by Hobbs, Bell and Robinson. To my shame, I did nothing other than to think how to stop this all becoming very ugly. That was a waste of time, I was sure.

The congregation dragged the two hucksters away until they reached the courthouse. It was going to be rough justice served here, I knew, and so I decided to turn a blind eye, go home and play with the dog.

Tarring and feathering is not a civilised punishment. First, the despicable pair were stripped fully naked and forced to watch some tar boil in a pot over a fire that had been put together by some farmers attending the funeral. Then it was poured over them and two cushions of feathers collected from the Butterwood Hatchery were emptied on top of their heads. My son Sam, who was too young really to be watching this cruelty, told me later, "Their screams were like the cries of a coyote. It got worse after that was all done, when the mob poured solvents, taken from Peter's tannery, over them to clean them up a bit. Their skin came off like wet paper. Then they were tied to a tree still looking like two dead blackbirds." He could not stop speaking. "Will you put them in the jail?" he said.

"The younger one had done very bad things to the three Englishmen. You've got to go see them and bring them home for dinner. I heard some things when they were talking to Dr Robinson. Their story sounds better than any Ma has told me. Better than any story I've ever been told."

It looked like I had no choice and I got up from my desk to look for the strangers. As I guessed, they were drinking in O'Malley's Tavern celebrating with drinks on the house provided by Paddy the barkeep. I had one, too, and then invited them and Henry Robinson home.

But first I had to look at and then rescue the poor creatures tied to the tree in front of the Courthouse. *Jail would be the safest place for them*, I thought.

Oliver, Charley and Jack came round on the dot at five o'clock. I made the introductions.

"This is my wife, Jane, who prepared the night's feast. These are my children. First is the eldest, Orion, who is now looking into buying and running the local newspaper. This is Pamela, who's a great musician, and finally young Samuel, my boy with a vivid imagination and lots of humour about him. He's only a twelve-year-old but he's seen some pretty gruesome things already in life. One man shot and killed in Main Street. Then there was the day he wandered into my office and right in front of his eyes was a dead body laid out cold, having just been left there before the inquest later in the morning. Worst of all there was his best friend's father shot in the back down by the river. Never found out who did it. Although, he was no great loss as he was the town drunk who used to beat his boy whenever the mood took him. A real nasty character was Pappy. And you can't help worrying about his kid. Sam brings him round some days and even now I can tell he'll either be a credit to us all or end up in front of my bench soon enough."

Sam went red-faced.

We sat and I asked the Englishmen their stories. Before they started, I assured them that the two conmen were in my jail and a trial would follow in the next few weeks.

They told their stories. And what stories they were. Starting at the end, they said how they arrived into Hannibal, thought the town was deserted, walked around and saw a big hall full of people singing. And they went in. To their shock they saw the man they called Monks. They'd chased him all the way from England and wanted justice for the friends and family that the creature, as they called him, had hurt, defrauded and murdered.

But it was the United States journey that had the rest of us enthralled. Especially young Sam, who laughed and cried while they were telling their tales. He even got his pen out.

Jack said, "Well, Mr Clemens, we've had an adventure or two. A black slave who was a musician and not a slave at all, who ended up in jail anyway. We've met Irish people escaped from the famine, gang leaders who beat, killed and blackmailed yet still went to Catholic confession every Sunday. Then there is the sorry tale of Injun Joe. And we heard stories of the most amazing kind about the two crooks calling themselves the duke and the king. Scams about drinking alcohol, cleaning teeth and feeling bumps on your head. The best of all being their tribute to William Shakespeare. I would have loved to have seen Monks' performance as King Lear, only to have been bettered by the entertainment he took part in today. Does tar and feathering make the three of us more than happy? No, sir. Ecstatic, I would say."

The other two nodded, grinning with tears of laughter in their eyes. Then they told the stories of their lives they had lived in London, where they first met. Fagin, Sikes and Nancy. You couldn't have imagined such people could exist.

"Never go to that place they call England, Sam," I said.

He just smiled.

The three of them were clearly a family and, as they said, they owed it all to a cesspit house in a place called Field Lane.

ANTOINE

My menus are rooted in the traditions of French cuisine. *Les plats du jour* can include *Escargots*, *Filet de Boeuf avec sauce Marchand du Vin et les champignons*, and also my definitive dish I call *Pommes de Terre Souffles*.

More recently, I've taken on the flavours and techniques of indigenous Creole cooking, with items like andouille smoked, gumbo and also a rice-based stew of sausage, chicken, shrimp and vegetables all seasoned with bell pepper, onion and celery. It is now my most popular dish. We now accommodate many important people and I hear much local and national gossip. I hope this evening will be no different.

Tonight's diners include a hero of the recent Mexican-American war, Quartermaster Ulysses S. Grant. During the crucial Battle of Monterey, he was the one who volunteered to carry a message to General Twiggs through streets occupied by Mexican forces. It was said in the local papers that, 'He ran the gauntlet, riding daredevil on the side of his horse with one foot hooked on his saddle and an arm around the neck of his horse'. What bravery.

I make it my business to know everything I can about my customers. So, I was intrigued to learn that Grant was predicted to become a high-flier in any future wars and maybe later in Washington. He would be accompanied tonight by the New Orleans Mayor, Abdiel Crossman. So, it would be the best table for them.

The other guests were regulars here. A doctor from the Charity Hospital called O'Reagan, *en famille,* along with our three resident Englishmen. The Irish ones were, of course, not the less desirable (and poor) famine exports though, as so many were in the city now. Then there was the pair I would have refused to entertain if I'd not been such a coward. Archie Murphy, the somewhat suspect 'businessman', had booked with his wife. "Dining for a special anniversary," he had said. Finally, a small party of four from *The Daily Orleanian.* That meant another full complement in the restaurant tonight. I was proud to have become the respected owner of a restaurant increasingly being used as a political salon. I had come a long way from my life in Marseille.

I opened *pensione Antoine* with my wife, Julie, to provide quality accommodation and good food for the elite in the city most welcoming to a Frenchman in the United States, New Orleans. I chose St Louis Street, between Bourbon and Royal, to set up my dream and it's now so popular I know a move to bigger premises must come soon.

Tonight's guests were booked for arrival between

six o'clock and seven thirty. The soldier and the mayor came first. Then the newspaper staff. After them was the O'Reagan party, including Oliver, Charley and Jack. It was clear to me the Irish don't always hate the English with a vengeance. Then again, I am a Frenchman who remembers tales from Waterloo, so what would I know?

They were all eating when the gang boss *et femme* arrived. I hope none of them recognised him as he was in smart clothing, and I had seated him at the very back of the room facing a wall. Otherwise, my reputation would plummet.

With every glass of wine, the Anglo-Irish table got a bit louder. It was obviously a farewell party for them. There was sobbing and laughter I could see and hear.

The good-looking blond one with piercing blue eyes called Oliver had one of those cutting British accents that can be clearly understood, even by a Frenchman. But as for his two friends it was still, I'm afraid, *j'ai pas compris*. Oliver spoke from the heart to all around the table, with tears in his eyes.

"You know how I started out life by being born in a workhouse begging for more gruel every day. And so, I would never have believed in my worst times there that one day I'd be sitting with best friends at a table eating the finest food I've ever tasted. So, my first toast is to *Monsieur Antoine*."

They raised their glasses in my direction.

"The second toast is to my fifth and best family, the O'Reagans, especially Michael for his good advice and the generous hospitality he has constantly given to three street urchins from London. Stop yawning, Jack, I've only got three more of these toasts to make. One of them is to our friends and family who were murdered, Charley's dad and our beloved Nancy, who saved me from many a beating by Fagin. If they are watching down on us from heaven above, then we toast you."

Jack then said (I think), "Sikes and Fagin will be looking up to us from Hell below, I'm sure."

Oliver carried on. "I'd like to drink a full bottle of whiskey to the town of Hannibal for tarring and feathering the scum called Monks. Let's hope he's soon keeping the company of his fellow rats, Fagin and Sikes. Last, but certainly not least, a toast to my best friends and brothers, Jack and Charley, who made my life worth living. And still do."

Then Dr O'Reagan spoke. "I have never met three more capable and personable young men in all my years of experience. Your parents would be proud of you. I am proud of you. But most of all, I'm going to miss you. *Sláinte.*"

The young lady nudged the one called Charley, who said, "You haven't quite got rid of me yet, Michael."

The whole table burst into more laughter and more tears. As did I.

The party was just about to break up when, to my horror, Archie Murphy went over to their table and said, "Paddy Connors sends his greetings from Hannibal. Well, not just greetings, more like a message really. He was happy to relate to me that the man called Monks met with an unfortunate accident in his jail cell in Hannibal. His neck had an encounter with a cut-throat razor. He thought you would be happy to hear he did not die quickly." Then he left not only with his wife, but also with a big smile on his face.

By the time all the customers had left it was eleven. Time for bed. I love this life.

"*Jusqu'à demain mes amies.*"

CHARLEY BATES:
STEAMBOATS

Dear Mary,

I'm writing this letter to say thank you for changing my life by sending me to the place you were born in the countryside. I had not lived a good life until then, I know. Pickpocket and sometimes a housebreaker. But never violent, even though I felt like murdering Bill Sikes after he beat poor Nancy to death.

When I heard Dad had been killed by that Chinese animal with his meat cleaver, I was not as sad or angry as I had been for Nancy. She was an innocent soul. Unlike Dad, who I had seen cudgel a man to death. He would say it was self-defence if he was here now, but it was more than that. Hatred for the Yellows, as he called the Chinese, is what it was more about, I think. But he did put an end to Monks and Fagin's child prostitution house. So, there was some good in him. I wish I could have told him so. And that I loved him.

I thought of Dad a lot while working in the fields every day at Althorp. Like I did about my old gang. Was what we did really wrong? The people we stole from were different from us. We did not really exist for them; we were the street mud under their fine boots. They did not care if we lived or died. We simply made a living by robbing them. It was our job.

Now I know so much more about what a tough life really means from being in the United States. At least in London we were never whipped or hobbled like black slaves are here. And we were never starved out of existence like the Irish under British rule. The ruling class of England is corrupt and has no compassion. It is not worthy of redemption, I now truly believe. That is why, big sister, I have decided to remain and live here. I feel no sense of pride in being called an Englishman like I did ten years ago, and I never will again.

It is not the only reason I want to stay in my new home of New Orleans. I have met a girl. Her name is Alice and we both have the same feelings for each other. It's my wish that one day she will become my wife, but the decision is hers to make... after I get the courage up to ask her.

I cannot list all the adventures I have had since my old friends Jack and Oliver came back into my life. They knew I was a wherryman before I became a thief, and now often call me Charley SteamBoats after the most popular transport on the Mississippi. That's a river I'd love to show you one day. It makes the Thames look like a piddle stream.

But my most important news is that mad dog Monks, the man responsible for Dad's murder and the child prostitution ring, has met his comeuppance. In style, too. He was tarred and feathered and then thrown into jail after we told the Justice of the Peace about his past activities. Actually, we went to visit him in his jail cell. Jack did not hold back as usual, saying some quite unrepeatable things for me to write in a letter, even to you. All I will say is, amongst many other things said, it involved the Dodge squeezing two rocks together on him hard at a man's most sensitive place. "That's if you have any!" he'd shouted. Oliver was much quieter but hurt the creature more, I think, by calling his mother "a whore without intelligence, morals or common decency. A woman who had raised such a thing should have been aborted herself at birth." I thought about saying nothing at all and just stabbing him with my knife, but I did not. Then the guilt I felt for the way Dad and I had parted... never having a chance to make up and say goodbye... caused a rage to build up inside me. And I spat at him three times through the bars.

We left him there wallowing in his memories of a squalid life lived without love or friendship ever playing a part. I wished him a painful death but not by the three of us. We are more than that, much more.

Monks had also made an enemy of a very important gang boss in his time over here. And his reach is long, as Monks found out. Justice was done and the creature ended up with a slit throat in his cell. Although nobody was charged, Mr Clemens, the Justice of the Peace we know well, suspects that Paddy Connors, the barman at O'Malleys, the local tavern, did the deed as he was seen outside the jail just before Monks was found dead. Archie Murphy's network of Irishmen did its job. And did it well. I shed no tears.

Well, that's all my news for now. Jack will fill you in with all the details I've missed out when he delivers this to you. Please give my love to Lil and Grandad Jimmy. I miss you all. Tell him I'll come back one day to see him. Maybe with a great-grandson?

With love,
Charley.

SIR CHARLES TANQUERAY

I was invited to one of the first planning meetings for the Great Exhibition, masterminded by the Prince Consort in Kensington Palace. The event itself was expected to take place in two years, but the meticulous Albert was making sure that all aspects of British intellectual life were represented now.

He had been inspired to mount this giant undertaking by Henry Cole, the editor of the respected *Journal of Design*. They had met at a meeting of the Royal Society for the Encouragement of Arts, Manufacture and Commerce, and decided an international exhibition aimed at the education of the public about British design, intellect and industry could – no, would – be of great importance to the economy. Such an ambitious aim meant entrepreneurs, scientists and engineers would be rubbing shoulders with representatives of the arts from sculpture, painting and literature.

Every marvel of our Victorian age would be there, including porcelain, ironwork, furniture, perfumes, pianos, firearms, fabrics, steam hammers and hydraulics. In other words, it was meant to be a showcase of pride for British intellectuals, innovation and manufacturing.

The event, I'm told, is going to be housed in a unique glass and iron conservatory, which will be called the Crystal Palace and located in Hyde Park.

My given task was to discuss how a scientific idea could be turned into commercial action, as exemplified by London Dry Gin and our LifeLong range of cordials. Obviously, I could not tell the Prince Consort the full story as it would reflect badly upon my reputation.

Nonetheless, I invited Jack and his particular friend Oliver Leeford along with me to present a more youthful enthusiasm about our ideas and achievements at Tanquerays. They were a bit overawed with the whole occasion, as indeed was I.

While I was setting up our table display of Zeus and Morpheus cordials, as well as our new fruit-flavoured dry gins and vodkas, I told Jack and Oliver to check out the competition we might have in two years' time.

While they were exploring, Lionel de Rothschild came up to me. He still sat on the LifeLong board and we saw each other at least twice a year. As always, we started talking about Frederick Sykes and what a loss he was to science.

"He would have loved to be here today," said Lionel. "Gone more than ten years now. Dead because of an opium dealer and a deranged, evil fool."

"At least Monks is dead himself now," I added, "but there'll be no justice for the Lascar, I think, unless he was killed in the Opium War."

"Another one may not be too far off, I hear from my government contacts," Lionel replied. "They're desperate, by all accounts, to find a diversion for the public to prevent any attacks on the monarchy here, like in the Austrian Empire and the German Confederation. Her Majesty still thinks of those countries as family members because of her Teutonic roots. I'd be surprised if Pam and Russell don't contrive another Opium War with China to focus republican minds."

Jack and Oliver came back very excited, *bubbly*, I thought, after they told me what they had seen. They had met an American called John Mathews who was the inventor of a compact apparatus for making carbonated water. He called them soda fountains and you could add flavourings like dandelion, sarsaparilla, and any fruit pulp.

That was not all. They also met Samuel Colt, who showed them his handheld range of revolver guns. Then they saw the exact electric telegraph that had helped, a few years back, to catch the Paddington Station killer, who had murdered his mistress and then caught a train but was followed by police after they received an instant telegraph message at his destination.

"And there are going to be some real steam engines there, too," said Jack. "We'll have to come more than once to see it all, especially the biggest diamond in the world that the queen is loaning."

Before we were formally introduced to the prince, I spoke to them both and told them to calm down.

Jack was all a bubble, though. "Is it true, Charles, the prince's father was the brother of Queen Victoria's mother?

Even my poor excuse for parents would have smiled at that."

I told him to shut up or he'd be looking for another job tomorrow.

Soon our host arrived and was very knowledgeable about our products, he said, because the mother of Her Royal Highness had been most impressed by the effects of Morpheus. So much so that she felt official recognition was deserved.

"Of course, the Duchess of Kent meant a knighthood. But I think my wife would be less inclined to celebrate Mother's Ruin, as she calls it, I'm sorry to tell you."

I thanked him and said all our futures were in the hands of young people like Jack and Oliver. The consort nodded and was about to go when a person standing close by caught his attention.

"Dickens," he said, "come join us. Here is our future. From the look of them both, I would guess they have quite some exciting adventures to describe to you, unless you know about them already."

Epilogue

"God save the King. The Queen is dead."

King Edward VII sat down at his new desk in January 1901 and picked up a handwritten letter, which had been left on his correspondence pile by his equerry, the day his mother died. It was in her handwriting.

It began, *Darling Bertie*, and the contents changed his life. She wrote that her mother, also called Victoria, had told her the then Duke of Kent was indeed not her father – could not have been because they had not slept together in that way for a year before she had been born.

Victoria believed her mother. But nonetheless, she took the Crown and exiled both her and that lackey Conroy from Court, only allowing the dowager duchess back in three years later when the pain had subsided and her mother's infidelity was disguised as a bad dream never to be shared or recognised as real. It was also the year Queen Victoria married Prince Albert.

It did leave a dilemma for Edward, though. He was

not the rightful king. The inheritance line from William IV should have passed through the Duke of Cumberland, who had only become King of Hanover in 1837 and not King of England as well, like his father before him.

The true heir in 1901, then, was Ernest Augustus, Crown Prince of Hanover, 3rd Duke of Cumberland and Teviotdale. He was a good friend and supporter of Kaiser Wilhelm II.

Edward VII decided to burn his mother's letter.

Acknowledgements

Before I retired from front-line science a few years back, I decided I wanted to do two things in my retirement. One was to attend cooking classes around the world. But the coronavirus put paid to that. The second was to write a novel.

I was determined to wait until I had a good idea, though. Finally, one came to me through the ether... or morphine, in my case. I was laid up in a hospital bed sans TV, Wi-Fi, books and visitors because of COVID restrictions.

Out of the 3G, I came across a book print from *Oliver Twist* illustrating a character called Charley Bates, who was a pickpocket for Fagin. *Who is he?* I thought. *Never heard of him.*

So, I checked Charley out, especially Dickens' description of his future, becoming a grazier of all things. Next, he described the fate of the despicable half-brother of Oliver. Dead in a jail in the USA! How might and why might that happen? Most importantly, whodunit?

Field Lane was born out of those questions, which resolved themselves in my mind as a collision between fictional characters living by the Thames and along the banks of the Mississippi.

But the bizarre idea that came to me then was, what if these fictional characters' influences were not only on our minds as readers of Dickens and Twain, but also on the contemporary world which the invented characters lived in?

After that, it turned out to be a fairly quick journey to get from random words in my head to the written novel you have just read. My greatest surprise doing my research was that many of the stories I came across were much wilder than any fiction I could possibly have had the mind to create. The plot uses and reflects many of those real goings on. With my dialogue, of course.

For everything, I owe a debt of gratitude to those who read my first attempts at constructing the metaphysical world of *Field Lane*. They helped shape the final novel with praise and constructive suggestions for improvement.

So, thank you: Hannah McCall, Paddy Feeney, Dan Crowley, Patsy and Kathleen Nyhan.

And, of course, the staff at Cork University Hospital and the South Infirmary Victoria University Hospital, Cork.

This book is printed on paper from sustainable sources managed under the Forest Stewardship Council (FSC) scheme.

It has been printed in the UK to reduce transportation miles and their impact upon the environment.

For every new title that Troubador publishes, we plant a tree to offset CO_2, partnering with the More Trees scheme.

For more about how Troubador offsets its environmental impact, see www.troubador.co.uk/sustainability-and-community